SHE IS VENGEANCE

KRISTIN MURDOCK

CONTENTS

Preface   vii

Sally's Sea Change   1
Winner: Scarlett Stiletto Awards Second Prize, 2010 /
Winner: Most Satisfying Retribution, SS Awards, 2010

A Beginner's Guide to French   19
Winner: Elyne Mitchell Award, 2016

Death On The Books   26

Plenty More Fish   44
Winner: Most Satisfying Retribution, Scarlett Stiletto
Awards, 2019

Cat People   62

Revenge Takes The Cake   82
'Winner: Body in the Library, Scarlett Stiletto Awards,
2020

Loose Ends   86

A Death In The Family   102

The Irony of Silence   120
Winner: Body in the Library, Scarlett Stiletto Awards,
2020

See The Light   138

Giving It Your Best Shot   154

Chinese Whispers   158

Dear Reader   177

'In revenge and in love woman is more barbaric than man is.'

FRIEDRICH NIETZSCHE
Beyond Good and Evil

PREFACE

Growing up in regional South Australia and sharing a birthday with 'Queen of Crime', Agatha Christie, Kristin Murdock is an multi award-winning writer.

This collection of short stories has strong, female protagonists.

"One of the joys of writing is being able to empower characters, especially female ones, to take charge of their own lives and outcomes," Kristin says.

Published as a Young Adult author (Bad Boys – Pan Macmillan) and contributing to three crime anthologies, Scarlett Stiletto (The Second Cut, The Eleventh Cut and The Twelfth Cut), Kristin is currently working on a crime series based in different locations in Australia.

SALLY'S SEA CHANGE

WINNER: SCARLETT STILETTO AWARDS
SECOND PRIZE, 2010 / WINNER: MOST
SATISFYING RETRIBUTION, SS AWARDS,
2010

In the beginning, Sally only explored the sandy curve of Burner's Beach as a way to avoid Michael.

Their trip from Adelaide had deteriorated from a spacious, double lane highway to a gravelly snake-like track that sloped its way to the base of sheer limestone cliffs. Escaping from the car, Sally found that the camping area, sandwiched between towering, scorched rock faces and a seductive lapping of waves, was heavy with oppressive heat. The long journey finished with the stress of erecting the heavy, cumbersome camper trailer.

Fortunately, Michael had invited friends on his big adventure and Sally expected his moodiness to be diffused in the social atmosphere. Their conversations tended to be brief and snappy these days. Michael had a way of muttering quietly, causing Sally to strain to hear until she realised he was spouting more sarcasm, primarily about her weight.

They were temporarily alone in the camping ground, accompanied only by low, shrubby trees and a damaged, green sign indicating the trees had been planted a decade earlier by local school children. At opposing ends, drop toilets stood like corrugated iron bookends.

Sally, arms aloft, steadfastly clutched the corner of the canvas annexe. She watched her husband's dark head leaning into a trailer, one hand frantically delving into a box of rattling junk while the other swiped sweaty hair from his forehead.

"See if you can hold on to that properly while I find the rope," he said, his flinty, brown eyes attacking her from beneath dark brows.

There had been a time when Sally fancied Michael's eyes as melted chocolate; warm, soft and comforting. He'd thought it cute at the time ("how sweet", she seemed to remember was his pun).

When she reminded her husband of it recently, he smirked.

"Trust you to be thinking of chocolate."

Sally tipped her head backwards, stretching her aching neck and searching the air for a hint of coolness. Beyond the hump of sand, heat shimmered in waves on the horizon, contorting the blueness of the sea into hypnotic curves. To the east, large clumps of rock rose awkwardly out of the water; jagged reddish-brown chunks seemingly thrust sideways into the seabed, the gentle sea caressing them softly.

Michael was still clattering amongst the contents of his poorly packed drawer (which he claimed was, somehow, Sally's fault) while Sally's arms began to prickle with pins and needles. The echo of a car's engine broke the silence, its noise resounding along the narrow cliff track, which was the only way into the camp ground.

"Sounds like Kate and Tony," Sally commented hopefully.

"Or Geoff and Amanda," he countered.

Michael stretched upright and brushed dirty hands over his red board-shorts, bought especially for the occasion. He peered expectantly around the edge of the camper but as yet no vehicle had appeared.

"My arms are going to sleep," Sally said.

"Let it down then."

He spoke dismissively and walked to the uneven camp track looking expectantly along the narrow road. "I'll see if the others have a spare rope."

Michael's interest was now in the arrival of their friends. Mentally he had already chosen the place they should park their caravans, with, in his opinion, best access to the beach. He'd also planned where the communal barbecue should be placed, as Michael and Sally had no room to bring one of their own.

Sally stretched and massaged the blood back into her arms. A silver four-wheel drive, with caravan bouncing behind, appeared around the bend. As it rattled into camp, a cloud of silvery gulls flew up from the rocks.

Michael ran a hand across his head and folded up the collar of his polo shirt. Sally took secret delight at the tiny thinning patch that was taking shape in his once thick hair.

"I might go cool my feet," she said.

Michael turned and muttered disinterestedly.

"Yeah, sure, love."

He closed the distance between them and clapped one hand on her rear end, squeezing a handful of flesh.

"Perhaps you should take a walk?"

Sally looked down as she slipped on her thongs, momentarily studying the chubby feet that protruded from the straps. Well practised, she ignored Michael's jibe and walked the short path to the beach. In a matter of seconds, she was treading the cooler, yellowish sands of Burner's Beach.

While one end of the beach abutted the scattered rocks that reared from the ocean, the western end of the beach yawned its way into a hazy distance. A matted web of scrubby vegetation came to the sand's edge, which was pristine, thanks to the laws of the local conservation park.

Water lapping her ankles, Sally leaned over and immersed her hands in the cool salty ocean. The reflection of a sad face framed by cropped, blondish hair was contorted by the water and typically Sally's focus was on the flab that oozed over the waist of her board shorts.

She wasn't looking forward to the intimate laughter from the perfect couple, Kate and Tony, or from Michael's work-mates, Geoff and Amanda. Sally stood up and viewed the sandy, endless curve of land where persistent waves had left a lace of wispy seaweed and a random smattering of shells at the high-water line. She inhaled; the air was sharp and intoxicating. On impulse, Sally stepped out of the water and began to walk west.

She wished she had taken her iPod from the car, but she ran her favourite tunes through her head instead; after all, she knew them word for word. What a blessed relief after Michael's company on the drive from the city!

Meryl Streep belting out the numbers from Mamma Mia was just the boost she needed right now. Who couldn't love the Greek Islands where white-washed houses clung to the cliffs and feisty, cheerful women lived beneath perfect blue skies? Now, that was a holiday!

The white arc of Burner's Beach soothed and relaxed Sally as she got her thoughts in order. It was no easy physical effort though, trudging along the soft sand, making Sally fully aware of the extra twenty kilos she had added since her last holiday with Michael. That had been years before, a spontaneous trip to New Zealand where they had hired a zippy, red car and explored the South Island. A lot had changed since then.

Eventually, Sally rested on the cool sand near the water's

edge. Looking back to the green brim of their camper trailer that poked above the low trees, Sally realised she hadn't walked very far at all.

About now, Kate and Tony would be ceremoniously popping their luxurious pop-top and breaking out the deck chairs and gin. Back in the real world, Kate and Tony lived opposite Sally and Michael, and Michael and Tony had an unacknowledged rivalry in all things material.

When Tony and Kate added a pergola to their house, Michael had added a (slightly larger) one to theirs. When Michael hired a landscaper to update the front garden, supposedly in the name of water efficiency, Tony had done the same thing.

When Tony showed off his latest pride and joy, a new caravan, Michael and Sally had gone across to christen its arrival with a gin and tonic. All the while, Michael was planning to purchase a more macho camper trailer, which eventually led to this camping trip to the edge of nowhere.

Sally refused to acknowledge her suspicions on why Geoff and Amanda were invited. Geoff worked with Michael at an insurance firm where Michael was technically Geoff's boss. Surprisingly he didn't dwell on the fact and, on the surface at least, it didn't seem to affect their relationship. However, Michael had made it clear that Geoff would need to keep a daily check on their clients. Difficult when there was no phone service at the base of the cliffs and it would require a drive back along the coast road to be in phone range. At the campsite, they were practically cut off from the world.

Unable to avoid the campsite or company any longer, Sally retraced her steps along the beach. She hoped to sneak a quiet gin and tonic with Kate and avoid Amanda, whose harsh, nasally voice and explosive laughter were at odds with the peace of the beach. Sighing, she broached the sandy hill.

"Hey Sally," Kate waved from the shade of her roll out awning, her blonde ponytail jiggling.

"We finally made it!"

Kate held up a glass and tinkled the ice invitingly. Sally grinned and stepped carefully between the spindly bushes to meet her friend. Michael and Tony were busy tethering a piece of canvas to a nearby tree.

From the corner of her eye, she could see Geoff and Amanda's caravan obscured behind a group of low trees.

"Hopefully she's blown away in the breeze," Kate whispered.

Sally laughed, thinking of Amanda's unbelievably thin figure.

"Don't worry about her Sal," Kate added, sensing her friend's trepidation. "At least Geoff's good company."

Kate was right on the money. Geoff was a great guy: genial, kind and with eyes the colour of spicy green olives. *Why do I always equate eyes with food?* Sally wondered briefly. But before she could consider it further, Kate thrust a drink in her hand.

"Here, get this into you before she floats past," she advised.

Sally only managed a sip of the fragrant mix before Amanda, sporting navy blue shorts and a pink singlet tiny enough to fit Kate's eight-year-old daughter, appeared before them like a piece of horrendously coloured driftwood.

"Hi girls," she paused and looked pointedly at Kate's glass. "Don't suppose I could have one?"

Kate smiled tightly before going back into her van.

"New shorts?" Amanda queried innocently, picking out a twig from her sandal.

Sally looked down at the shapeless blue material currently stretching harshly across her thighs.

"Never underestimate a fat woman," she quipped cheerily.

Sally studied the pattern of tracks left in the sand by a recently passing lizard. Inwardly, she swore at herself for making a comment that wasn't even relevant. It was a stupid defence mechanism she'd picked up somewhere.

Amanda smiled smugly at her. It was going to be a long week.

Later, when the sun had vanished into the haze of the distant point and the cool evening air had settled around them, the group circled their deckchairs beneath the awning of Kate and Tony's van.

"Top spot Michael," Amanda said approvingly. Her head swivelled to peruse the inky coolness that surrounded them. "There's not another soul for miles."

"Thought you'd like it," Michael replied with a cheeriness boosted by red wine. "You'll be able to do a few beach runs."

"I won't be straying far from camp," Amanda said, clasping one hand around her left ankle. "I strained my Achilles at the gym last week."

Usually, Sally didn't contribute much to small talk, often amazed how being overweight could make a person invisible. Suddenly though, she needed to be included.

"I thought I might walk up the beach every day."

"Good on you," Geoff commented from his deck chair, olive eyes on her as he sipped red wine.

Tony balanced a platter of biscuits and dips on his huge hands and offered them around the group.

"Don't think I'll worry too much," he commented chewing a wedge of cheese.

Kate slapped him on the leg as he went past. "You are so lazy, Tony Grafton."

"You still love me though, right?"

Amanda let out a trill of laughter. "You two make me sick," she said. "I need another drink. Anyone else?"

Michael straightened up in his chair. "Sure, I'll give you a hand." He turned to Sally. "Want one, love?"

Sally took in the sudden animation of his face, the smudged circle of red wine on his lips.

"No thanks, I might head off to bed."

Michael didn't take the hint and kissed her on the head like a child as she passed by. Geoff appeared deep in conversation with Kate and Tony and unconcerned as his wife vanished into the bushes with Michael. It was the last image Sally had as she listened to the rhythm of the waves and the slap of the canvas walls before eventually drifting off to sleep.

Sometime later, it seemed like hours, she abruptly awoke, aware Michael was still not beside her. Scrambling in the darkness she found her mobile phone and checked the time — 2:30 am.

Sally pulled on her track pants and cautiously opened the zip of the camper. Above her, a million stars shone with clarity enhanced by the pristine air of the beach. Two voices punctuated the perfect silence, accompanied by the occasional harsh peal of laughter. Sally saw two figures sitting close together on the beach, wine glasses angled into the sand on each side. With a now familiar weight settling in the pit of her stomach, Sally forced herself back into the camper.

The next night, it happened again, only this time, Sally saw Michael's arm snaking around Amanda's waist. Standing in the shadows of the bush, she became aware of another figure further along the sand. It was Geoff, his position betrayed by a glint of the dull moon on his glasses. For a moment, in shared silence, they caught each other's eye before Geoff melted back into the bushes.

Sally never expected it to affect her so much — finally seeing the proof of what she had suspected for so long. Angrily wiping away tears, she fought the urge to cross the sand and scream obscenities at her husband and the woman he now engaged in a lingering kiss. Wooden legs somehow propelled Sally back to the silent campervan where she leant on the canvas, stomach churning violently. Her fingernails clenched the fabric, embedding themselves. It was no use, Sally leaned into the nearest bush and vomited.

Michael was up before Sally the next morning but she decided not to seek him out. Instead, she threw on a voluminous old t-shirt of fluorescent orange and resumed her ritual pacing along the beach. The tranquillity helped galvanise her thoughts, and she was surprised how far she walked before turning back.

Near the campground path, Tony stood on the beach, surrounded by various tackle boxes and patiently dangling a fishing line in the water. Sally was amazed at her ability to offer false cheerfulness.

"Fish for tea?"

Tony grinned, dipping the rod as though just the mention of it had brought one on to the line. "That's Kate's plan," he said with a throaty laugh. "I think it might be easier to go to a seafood restaurant."

"Nice walk?" he added. "You're becoming a bit of a regular."

Sally breathed the crisp air, "It's soothing ... and so deserted."

"Well, you're not hard to see with that shirt on," Tony commented winding his reel slightly.

Funny how Michael thinks I'm invisible, Sally thought, clenching her hands to hide the sudden well of emotion.

Aware of a shape in her palm, Sally opened her fingers.

"Look at this," she said, revealing a toffee-coloured shell edged with softly speckled serrations. On finding it at the point,

Sally fancied the beach had offered a reward for her aching calf muscles and heavy heart.

"That's a cowrie shell. You don't find them very often. They're good luck you

know."

Sally curved her fingers protectively around the shell. *Good luck?* she thought. That was exactly what she needed.

"Where is everyone?"

"Kate's reading, I think. Geoff's gone along the road to find phone service so he can ring a client. Not sure about Amanda or Michael."

Sally nodded and knew Tony caught her sadness. She walked off abruptly, mind buzzing with what Michael and Amanda were up to, especially since he had sent Geoff off on work errands. Kate would hardly cramp their style either, once her nose was buried in a book.

Approaching the corner of the camper, Sally could hear voices from the table in their annexe.

"'Never underestimate a fat person,' she says." It was Tony, derisory and smug.

Amanda's laughter cut through her like a knife. Sally moved away, embarrassed by the ridiculousness of her own words.

She stumbled to Kate's van, finding her friend with her glasses perched on her nose and finger poised on the corner of the next page of her latest novel. The smile she offered quickly disappeared when she saw Sally's face.

"Sally, what's wrong?"

Sally squeezed into the narrow caravan seat. She pulled up the hem of her ridiculous fluoro shirt to wipe away her tears, not caring what was revealed beneath.

"Michael and Amanda." Their names were bitter in her mouth. "They're having an affair."

Kate was incredulous and shut her book with a jolt, the bookmark fluttering uselessly to the floor.

"You must be mistaken Sally," she said, though the truth of it all was plain on her friend's face.

"How do you know? How long?"

Sally shrugged, glad Kate believed her and that she wouldn't have to explain further.

"How do you know? Where are they?" Shocked, Kate stumbled over her words.

"I just know," Sally said with sudden calmness. "But she's not getting away with it that easily. He's my husband not hers."

"Does Geoff know? What can I do Sal?"

Sally looked at her dear friend who was normally so coherent and found it within herself to smile.

"Sorry Kate, I shouldn't have barged in here like an idiot but ... " she trailed off uncertainly.

Kate placed a hand on her shoulder, encouraging her to continue.

"Don't worry, I'll talk to Michael tonight. We can sort it out." Sally clutched the cowrie shell in her hand. "Wish me luck."

The confrontation with Michael was brief.

"Hi Hon, Amanda and I thought we might go out snorkelling and try to spear some fish. Geoff has all the gear we need. He thought Amanda could give it a go but he's not here so I might—" he broke off when he saw the chill in his wife's face. "What's up?"

Sally gripped the nearby table.

"I know you're having an affair with Amanda."

The conversation was mercifully quick and involved no shouting or tears, though, typically, Michael was on the defensive.

Half an hour later, Michael and Amanda could be seen

wading through the shallows brandishing snorkels and spears. Amanda turned and waved cheerily back to Kate and Sally who stood together on the shore.

Kate was unable to control herself any longer.

"What happened?" she hissed.

Closer to the water, Tony still sat doggedly on the beach with his line, accompanied by Geoff who cradled a beer in one hand.

Kate looked as though she would burst.

"Did you talk to him? Why are you letting them go off together?"

Sally laughed with unexpected lightness. "One question at a time."

"Sally!"

"Michael's promised to call it off. 'A stupid mistake,' he said."

Sally turned to her friend, absorbing the incredulous expression that twisted her face.

"I know you think I'm pathetic, Kate, but I'm willing to try and make things work." She straightened her shirt with a sigh. "Who else would have me?"

"Don't be ridiculous," Kate snapped. "You don't have to put up with this garbage."

"I know," Sally admitted. "Look, I really appreciate your support, but it's alright, really. I'm sorry I even bothered you with it. Michael doesn't want to make a scene now; he'll talk to her in the morning when Geoff's out checking on clients so ... "

"Should Tony and I make ourselves scarce?"

Sally placed a comforting hand on Kate's shoulder.

"No, really, I just want this all to be over and for things to go back to normal. If you disappear in the morning it will seem a bit odd. Michael thinks Amanda will freak out so it's probably better if you are around."

"If you say so." Kate wasn't convinced. "Will he really do it?"

Sally sighed but put on a brave smile.

"He promised."

Morning dawned bright and clear as it had all week, with barely a breath of wind to ripple the placid water. Sally set off walking in her usual old, fluorescent number: a relic from the eighties. She wore her iPod and sang along to Mamma Mia, toes digging into the damp sand to the tune of "Dancing Queen". She intended to be in the best mood possible when she returned to camp.

Tony, despite several unsuccessful attempts at fishing, set up again with typical cheerfulness, determined to catch something. As usual Geoff had driven off to phone the insurance clients.

Determined to stay low profile when the inevitable confrontation between Amanda and Michael loomed, Kate busied herself by tidying the van.

Sally kept the cowrie shell in her pocket, counting on its ability to bring good luck. Absently, she rubbed it like a magic lamp, her eyes focused on the distant point of land. She decided to stay positive. After all, today was a new beginning.

About forty minutes later, back in her caravan, Kate prepared a cup of coffee for Tony who had returned from the beach for his ritualistic morning cuppa. Kate was considering whether to tell Tony of the complications in the lives of their friends when an agonised shriek from outside caused her to spill milk all over the tiny sink. It was unmistakably Amanda, but instead of her usual laughter, it was a harsher, more urgent scream. Tony and Kate looked at each other. Though Kate had promised not to intervene, she had never anticipated such a reaction.

Tony, sensing the urgency in the scream, was already out of

the van and running purposefully in the direction of Geoff and Amanda's caravan.

Kate and Tony appeared at the door at the same time. It was flung back open and Amanda's face, contorted in horror, loomed over the naked body of Michael, crumpled on the unmade bed with the shaft of a spear sticking vertically out of his chest. Unseeing eyes stared at the ceiling with frozen surprise as a red stain spread on the white quilt beneath him.

I didn't think she would take it so badly, Kate thought ridiculously.

Tony swiftly snatched the spear-gun from where it lay on the floor by Amanda's feet. Stupid, really, as it was now rendered useless. Grabbing his phone, Tony stabbed his fingers at the emergency number before realising he had no service.

Amanda had morphed into a state of shock. She pushed Kate aside, stumbled down the van steps and ran haphazardly over to the beach. Once there, she started wading frantically out to sea, water splashing up wildly on to her skirt.

Determined not to let her escape, Kate followed the hysterical figure into the water. In the distance, Kate could see Sally's orange figure walking slowly back to the camp, blissfully unaware the woman who was having an affair with her husband had just murdered him.

ONE YEAR LATER

Sally relaxed on the blue tiled terrace and peered out at the Mediterranean.

One of the old Greek ladies from the bakery had just delivered the most spectacular fresh bread and now joined her on the terrace, sipping iced tea. Sally was now accustomed to the fact that Sophia typically wore black, much like the feisty Greek women in Mamma Mia.

"You have done wonders to this place," Sophia intoned slowly, unfamiliar with English until recently.

Sally leaned back into her chair and smiled. *Never under estimate a fat woman.*

Odd how those words still found their way unbidden to Sally's lips. In fact, they had entered her head several times since the funeral and intense police investigation.

It was stress that eventually caused her to leave Australia, or so Kate and Tony said, as they waved her off from the airport three months ago. After all, who would want to stay behind and live with such memories? Especially with the papers still featuring follow up stories on Amanda's trial and impending incarceration. Unbelievably, Amanda's now sallow face continuously vowed her innocence. Everyone agreed Sally had suffered enough. First the affair, then the murder ...

Sally looked around her new home. Luckily, being in the insurance game, Michael had always insisted on a hefty life insurance policy for himself.

Kate still phoned occasionally. She had been a kind and trusting friend through it all, believing every word Sally said about the conversation she had with Michael that day at Burner's Beach. In reality, the snake had no intention of calling off his affair with Amanda. It didn't matter really, as long as Kate believed that Michael had intended to.

And dear Tony, such a creature of habit with his fishing and morning coffee break. Once he saw Sally set off for her walk, his use was over. It was a bonus that stupid Amanda had led Kate back to the beach after Michael was dead and she saw Sally striding back from the point. Except it hadn't been her, had it?

Sally stretched her feet on the tiled floor. *You have to love a perfect alibi.*

"Tell me about the beaches in Australia?" Sophia asked, always eager to hear of Sally's faraway homeland.

"They're beautiful," Sally remembered fondly. "You should visit sometime."

"I see you walking on our beaches," Sophia padded her rounded stomach. "That's why you stay so thin. I think I eat too much bread."

Sally smiled; some habits were hard to break. She still occasionally wore the orange fluorescent t-shirt for old time's sake, one of the exact pair she had in her cupboard.

Amazing, Sally reflected often, how very unobservant people were when they saw things from a distance.

Thoughtfully, Sally sipped her tea. She would never forget the look in Michael's eyes when she shot him through the heart with the spear-gun that still conveniently bore Amanda's prints.

Never underestimate a fat person.

It had been amazingly simple, a matter of hiding in the bushes a little way along the beach and hurrying back through the patchy scrub. Waiting amongst the branches by the van, she shrouded her hands in plastic bags to disguise any prints and felt the weight of the spear-gun that had been left resting against a tree. The soft moans and gentle movement emanating from the caravan caused Sally's anger to fester and boil beyond redemption. Michael was so disgustingly predictable.

As hoped, Amanda exited the van to visit the drop toilet. With stealthy movements uncommon in a woman of her size, Sally entered the caravan and swiftly finished a chapter in her life. She was out and running back through the bushes before Amanda had even unbolted the toilet door.

Sally nibbled slowly at a biscuit. She still harboured slight regret that Kate and Tony saw Michael like that. They had unknowingly been such an integral part of the plan, but the horrified look on Tony's face when she returned to camp after completing her apparent walk, her face slightly reddened from exertion, still brought about a twinge of guilt. Still, after months of pretending to be useless and downtrodden, she felt she had played the part of the shattered wife to perfection.

Then, poor Tony had driven out to contact the police and come across Geoff, supposedly returning from making phone calls along the road that bordered the scrub. Little did Tony know it was a surprisingly short walk through the trees to the beach near the point. And who would have thought she and Geoff fitted into the same size shirt? While Geoff ground the sand from his shoes into the car floor, Tony was so focused on the tragedy back at camp that he could hardly bring himself to speak.

In the back room of the white washed Greek house, a wireless speaker was clicked into life and the Mamma Mia soundtrack was dispersed by whirring ceiling fans throughout the open house. Sally looked over at Sophia. How patient the Greeks were not to tire of Meryl and her friends.

Instead, Sophia's focus was on Sally's neck.

"That shell, is that from one of your Australian beaches?"

Sally's hand slid to her neck where the good luck cowrie, made into a necklace soon after Amanda's conviction, sat between her jutting collarbones.

"Yes, I found it last summer."

"Beautiful," the woman nodded as she stood up. "Well, thank you for the tea. I must get back to the bakery."

Sally smiled and waved. Her other hand traced the fingers that now rested her shoulder. The skin was cool and still slightly damp from the shower.

Sally looked up and smiled at the man she should have married in the first place and not carried on a two-year affair with first.

She had lost weight since that fateful camping trip all right, about 95 kilos to be exact. They had laughed about that in bed the other night. It was the maximum kill weight suggested on the spear, and by the way Michael had collapsed like a sack on the bed, that would have been about correct.

Sophia waved as she walked through the door.

"Goodbye Mrs Sally, Goodbye Mr Geoff."

Sally squeezed her palm around the cowrie shell as had become her habit. It had certainly been good luck, just like Tony said.

Sally smiled up at her new husband.

The shell had been the second-best thing she took home from the beach last summer.

A BEGINNER'S GUIDE TO FRENCH

WINNER: ELYNE MITCHELL AWARD, 2016

At the funeral, handfuls of golden, plump grains of wheat were sprinkled like rain onto Neil Pratt's coffin; a quaint country tradition, performed to a background of mumbled farewells and a complexity of individual memories. On the peak of the windswept hill near Mudgella, Neil was duly interred among many who had once been his friends: other small-town locals, who in life had discussed local footy scores on the grubby step outside the bank or complained about the latest cereal harvest over a beer at the pub.

Like a rudderless boat, Gail was buffeted by the persistent waves of condolence that were repeatedly offered for her husband whose coffin rested on some sort of contraption that was poised to lower him into the fertile ground he so loved. It was unnerving for Gail to unclench her jaw and formulate a response. After fifty years as a sidekick, she preferred to blend into the background of any melodrama, not be the one in the spotlight.

So how the hell did she deal with it?

Not for the first time, Gail regretted that she and Neil

hadn't produced children. She wanted someone to share her life with; dilute the sadness, multiply the happiness. What was the point of regrets though? *If only*, the two saddest words in the universe.

According to Doc Naylor, Neil hardly felt a thing. Heart attack. Jumped out of the ute in the scrub paddock, about to check the new crossbred lambs and *bam!* 68 years of existence slowly disintegrated into the dirt of Sunset Farm. And Gail, at that moment, stretching her legs at the new senior's exercise class in town, was none the wiser.

She hadn't mentioned the class to Neil, but it didn't take long for the only policeman in town to locate Gail. Helen, at the general store, knew almost everyone's routine, and quickly directed Constable Mayer on where to go. When he entered the small, sweaty room that jutted from the side of the Mudgella Town Hall, Gail was flat on her back and performing bicep curls, thinking about how Neil never saw the importance of scheduled fitness.

"Moving a mob of sheep is plenty of exercise." He was fond of grumbling. As for classes on the internet (back when it was all new), well, Neil couldn't see the point in that either.

The crowds of mourners had fragmented into small groups, turning away from the freshly turned earth of the gravesite and returning to their cars.

Gail felt tears pricking awkwardly in the corner of her eyes. Clasping the iron frame of the cemetery gate, she found the metal, warmed by the afternoon sun, to be strangely comforting. She longed to be one of the anonymous human flow, drifting back to their vehicles on a receding tide of sorrow.

There was a warm symbiotic relationship among these people; so many of them were related to each other in one way or another. Gail knew this was not found in the city where no one dared meet the eyes of another.

Sue Thorne, proprietor of the Mudgella Post Office, met Gail's eyes with her own, their blue depths glistening slightly. How many 'Stock Journals' had Sue poked in their mail box over the years? What an odd thing to think of. Gail held Sue's pale hand briefly until the younger woman moved on. A brief respite before being subjected to the next wave of sympathy.

When Gail came to Mudgella over fifty years ago, she had been a bright-eyed teacher from Adelaide, fresh from years of learning, who wanted to share her knowledge with others. Neil, a dark, brooding farmer from the largest property in the district, had swept her off her feet. In the whirlwind, Gail caught the envious eyes of the other girls in town when Neil drew her onto the sawdust sprinkled dance floor. Back in the day when people danced.

Blessedly, the line of well-wishers dwindled, until Gail remained in an uncomfortable threesome with the minister and funeral director. Her body slumped in exhaustion. No surprise, as she had barely slept since Constable Mayer had found her at the exercise class, sweaty and breathless, while her husband's body was being transported to the hospital morgue. Always in charge, Neil had just enough time to dial the ambulance apparently. Gail wasn't surprised.

But, exhausted or not, her presence was required at the Mudgella Tigers Footy Club, the site of every local wake. Steering the ute back into Mudgella, Gail found an ironic smile play on her lips. Country life! One minute you're helping out a local family whose elderly member has passed away, next minute you become that elderly member! Time had a way of moving on, however stagnant it feels at the time. Gail entered the clubroom and obediently cradled the milky coffee that some young Mum, head bowed, had slipped into her hand.

Trestle tables were laden with homemade baking. In spite of the occasion, Gail took note of the velvety texture of the rasp-

berry cheesecake slice. A cooking class to learn about such delicacies had always been on her bucket list. But there was never
the time, nor, as Neil said, was there the necessity, particularly
when his mother's CWA cookbook lay in the kitchen drawer,
spattered with years of flying cake mix that it wore as a badge of
honour.

Four o'clock. Surely an appropriate time to leave?

"You look tired," someone said.

"So drained," noted Greg Carpenter, placing one hand on
her arm. He was the local stock agent, clad in his pin-striped
work-shirt; the death of Neil Pratt apparently not warranting
an entire day off.

"What will you do now?" many asked aloud, puzzled that
quiet, mousy Gail Pratt would consider staying out at the farm
alone. Gail smiled appropriately. Little did they know, she had
been on her own for years.

Gail placed her empty cup on the counter. An empathetic
young mother, counting down the minutes to the school bus,
snatched it up efficiently, dipping it in a sink of lukewarm,
soapy water.

Finally, Gail made her escape, steering the rattly ute down
the familiar dusty road to home and solitude.

Despite what others predicted, back at the huge homestead,
things didn't appear quiet or lonely. Neil and Gail had barely
spoken for years. Gail looked across the paddock where sheep
grazed on last year's wheat stubble. In her mind she searched
for the right description. Calm. Yes, that was precisely the right
word.

Opening the screen door, a whoosh of cool air rushed inside
from the shaded bullnose veranda. Gail propped a spider-
webbed work boot against the door to wedge it open. Butch,
their overworked border collie, lifted his head from his fluffy
paws with an expression Gail fancied was surprise. Neil

detested the doors open in the evening and the way it allowed the day's accumulated warmth to escape.

Her footsteps echoed along the hallway on the way to their bedroom. Sitting on the long, superfluous double bed, Gail slid a bedside drawer open, long fingers moving deftly through the jumble of sensible brown socks. Sensible, according to Neil, as they hid the dirt from working in the sheep yards, allowing Gail to whizz into town at a moment's notice and still look presentable. A short walk to the kitchen and the practical bundles were tipped firmly into the bin, except for one pair which bulged with awkward angles: a misshapen, oversized pair.

For years, Gail had successfully pilfered small amounts of money from her housekeeping allowance. Housekeeping? Who had that anymore? Once, Gail had mentioned it to a young girl from down the general store. She'd peered over her nose ring and looked at Gail like she was a quaint relic from a bygone age.

Trouble was, Gail was never permitted to get off the farm much or to learn new things. Permitted? She visualised the amused look from that same young girl. No need for such garbage, according to Neil. Waste of time and money.

Gail shook the sock and bundles of tightly rolled notes tumbled onto the kitchen counter. Pacing across the polished floorboards, Gail rifled through the kitchen drawer; hidden beneath her long-gone mother-in-law's CWA cookbook, Gail withdrew a glossy catalogue.

Paris. Happy tourists smiled from the cover and Gail found herself smiling back at their two-dimensional images, but without the blandness she had perfected over time.

If she and Neil had owned a computer (but, of course, that wasn't necessary), Gail would have flicked through the tour itinerary as she often did at the local library. The Eiffel Tower,

Montmartre, Toulouse; exotic colours and the promise of decadent aromas, far removed from the paddocks and sheep yards.

Her newfound freedom meant Gail didn't shift the money or travel brochure from the counter. Instead, she removed a recently purchased bottle from the fridge and decadently poured herself a wine — for no reason at all! From beneath a pile of newspapers in the corner (you never know when they may come in handy according to Neil), Gail withdrew another carefully hidden brochure.

She turned the pages, feasting her eyes on the list of classes, their names rolling decadently around Gail's imagination — reiki, Facebook, scrap booking, tango; a virtual check list of everything Neil deemed unnecessary. With delicious lightheartedness and the dryness of wine on her lips, Gail pencilled a ring around her selections. She chose a pertinent one for her first choice — 'A Beginners Guide to French'.

Old habits die hard. Gail nearly slid the brochure back into its hiding place in the drawer, before remembering there was no need for secrets anymore. Since Neil's heart attack, she hadn't even wiped down the glass door of the oven, and she felt ridiculously smug about it.

Gail sipped her wine thoughtfully. If Neil had been observant at any stage over their fifty years together, he may have come across that list of classes and noticed the barely visible pen dot that marked the one course she had secretly attended ("I've got a mammogram love, need to go to the city, women's stuff.").

'Eating for a Healthy Heart'.

Gail had listened intently to the lecturer and made a pertinent list of notes before returning to the farm. She had memorised the health tips and proceeded to...

Do. The. Exact. Opposite.

Well, for Neil anyway. Plenty of saturated fats and fried

food, and he didn't complain once. He had even made a joke about his expanding waist line over the last few months. Gail had smiled indulgently.

Of course, she could never be sure whether she had contributed to his ultimate collapse or not, with his family history of heart disease and all, but she couldn't be sure she hadn't either. Did she accelerate the ultimate scenario along a few years? Was it technically murder, or manslaughter at the very least?

She leant back in the wooden chair and nonchalantly rested one foot on the table. With Neil gone, Gail had years of freedom to ponder over that. Perhaps there was a series of legal lectures where she could learn such details?

Gail sipped the last of her wine, picked up a pencil and thoughtfully placed a ring around one more course: 'Dealing with Guilt'. It was scheduled for the day before she flew out to Paris.

First up though was 'A Beginner's Guide to French'.

C'est la vie

DEATH ON THE BOOKS

F ace ashen and feathered by tendrils of bleached blonde
hair, she was trembling with exertion as she ran from the
building toward me. I was frantically juggling a rain-jacket,
keys, a handbag and my hastily packed lunch. And you might
find this surprising, but I wasn't initially shocked when Harriet
breathlessly announced that there was a body in the library.

Behind Harriet, the wide door of Bennelong District
Library closed in a silent and unhurried arc. Harriet clutched
at my arm, causing the lentil salad to tip on the ground, legumes
settling like tiny islands in a muddy puddle. Ideally, they
should have landed on concrete, but the pavers hadn't turned
up, leaving the approach to the building rather muddy and
decidedly non-library like. I took a deep breath, forced a smile
and looked at my frazzled co-worker. "Of course there's a body
in the library," I said calmly. "It's Medical History Week. The
committee was here last night setting up the display."

Which, on a brighter note, meant their damned junk was
out of our tea room! Mannequins, old style nurse's uniforms

and antique medical equipment had been multiplying and filling our staff room for weeks. The enthusiastic members of the Library Board sometimes forgot that the library was a business, with employees who needed their personal space. Just last week, Harriet and I had been forced to rest our morning cuppas on plastic kidney bowls that had been deposited onto our desk.

I squatted down, tucking my shirt in modestly behind my folded legs and began to scrape up the sodden sprouts. Heaven forbid a customer should slip on my healthy lunch and sue the industrious Library Board. That would really make the Chairman happy!

Harriet knelt down with the ease of the young and began picking up runaway sprouts. Her name tag shook on her heaving chest.

"No, Jenny, a real body."

I had realised Harriet was prone to exaggeration since she started as my assistant almost a year ago. This time though, there was a set to her jaw that made me forget my sodden salad and register the horror in her blue eyes.

"What do you mean?"

"It's Mr Dewey," Harriet said, voice quavering slightly. "He's dead."

Barry Dewey, the Chairman of the Library Board, who I had just been mentally cursing in my head, was dead in our library? Barry was pompous, balding and arrogant and strangely predestined to become chairperson of a library board. After all, he had the same last name as the creator of the Dewey decimal system, the time-honoured technique of cataloguing library books. Barry regularly swanned about our bookshelves, favouring the non-fiction section, pointedly rearranging the odd book that had strayed from his personal and strictly maintained 'Dewey Dewey' decimal system. And now, after an evening of arranging the medical display, his expanding girth and poor health had presumably led to a heart attack in his beloved Bennelong Library. If not so shocking, it would be poetic!

I checked my watch. It was five to nine, meaning members of the Bennelong public, including students from the nearby Area School, would be wandering over any minute. Lunch forgotten; I rose decisively to my feet.

"Show me, Harriet. Are you sure he's dead? Did you call an ambulance?"

Harriet matched my quick pace into the library. Initially, everything appeared normal. The pre-set air conditioner hummed soothingly, the carpet around the borrowing desk was its usual smooth sea of blue. On my desk, by the window, were the flowers given to me by my ex-husband (would he ever give up?) for my birthday last week. I had turned 52. Barry Dewey had turned 58 the same day and had broken from his book inspections to loudly offer congratulations from aisle four. And now he was... I looked around. Where exactly was he?

A frame of morning sun glowed around the lowered blinds. On the opposite wall, an impressive reproduction of medical scenes had been assembled in the area usually reserved for new books: 'Medicine Through the Years'. It was just as the Library Committee had described to me. Three distinct displays showed a scene from the Middle Ages where a surgeon leant menacingly over a patient with a scalpel, a stiffly made-up Florence Nightingale and a modern-day operating room complete with a heart monitor and crisp sheets. Appropriately themed novels adorned the shelves alongside. Even in my quick evaluation, I could tell the Board had done their usual professional job at creating a reading theme for our customers.

"Where is he, Harriet?" I demanded. I had already hastily pressed three zeros on to the screen of my mobile phone.

From Harriet's frozen demeanour a trembling finger managed to emerge, pointing to the middle display.

In my hurried scan of the library, I had expected to find Barry lying on the floor, hand clutched to his chest, I had overlooked the authenticity of the body on the hospital bed from the Middle Ages. But now I focused on the supine figure; the greying hair and the flabby jowls were only too familiar. It was Barry Dewey, apparently naked and covered with a sheet.

"What the?" I stammered, but my words didn't hold the sarcastic humour of the high school students that were due any minute. "What happened?" I asked stupidly.

We edged closer. Never an attractive man, the thin sheet outlined every curvature of Barry's naked body. He had excessively hairy shoulders, and a flabby right arm hung from the side of the bed. On the floor of this staged operating theatre, Barry's clothes were flung in disarray. Beige trousers lay in a crumpled heap, with the impossibly spotless toes of his shoes poking out at obscure angles. His shirt and singlet were at the others end of the gurney and, most disturbingly, his navy underwear hung from the arm of the mannequin doctor.

But the killer — quite literally — was the old-fashioned syringe; a metal contraption with huge diameter and a thick glass tube. It protruded like a fence post from Barry's eye socket, where a gelatinous substance lay oozing on his skin. My stomach lurched alarmingly. Even the stiff doctor mannequin that loomed over him looked shocked. This was no heart attack!

The Bennelong Police Force consists of two men, Sergeant Michael Roach and Constable Pete Herring. Harriet and I had only recently discussed how amusing it was that our police station had a fish and an insect in charge. Particularly apt when one considered Pete Herring's high cheek bones, angular face and spectacularly pointy nose; the only thing missing was the gills! Michael, on the other hand, was nothing like a roach; he was tall with sandy hair and a quick, disarming smile, quite handsome really. But, as he is my son-in-law, I could be biased!

By the time they arrived, Harriet and I had locked out the public and were waiting at the returns desk with two cups of strong coffee. Harriet was calmer now, though I noticed she kept her gaze steadfastly on me and away from the scene of Barry's demise. But then, I wasn't so keen to look either!

It didn't take long for the crime scene tape to transform our usually quiet Monday morning library session. Crowds of curious locals gathered outside, many of whom I'd never seen near the place! Who needs the internet when the small-town grapevine gets active?

"We should have a murder here more often," Harriet commented drily, watching as Pete Herring spoke calmly to the assembled crowd.

"Murder?" I echoed quizzically, sipping my coffee. Although it was, of course. Barry hadn't undressed, lay down on the ancient operating table, thrust a syringe in his left eye and died of natural causes!

Michael looked very handsome in his police uniform. As he strode purposefully through the door, I could see once again why my daughter, Samantha, had fallen for him in the first place.

He offered Harriet and me a broad smile that was both comforting and professional.

"Well, Jenny, didn't expect to be seeing you until you dished up tonight's roast pork."

With my daughter away in Melbourne, I had taken pity on Michael and offered to cook him dinner. I thought of the leg of pork currently defrosting in my fridge at home. My day's initial attempt at health food looked to be heading rapidly downhill by dinner time.

"Might have to take a raincheck on that," I said. "I imagine you'll be kept busy for a while."

"Barry's over there," Harriet said, as though he was skulking between the shelves and efficiently lining up the spines of books.

"Right, let's see," Michael said. Pete came through the library door. "Make sure they're locked," Michael ordered.

Pete shook the doors to check before joining us at the medical display, which was thankfully out of sight of the crowd outside. He nodded in greeting.

"I called Jeremy Dozer, the coroner from Manton. He should be here shortly," Michael informed us.

"I called the plumber," Pete said.

That seemed an odd thing to say under the circumstances.

"Police station's flooded, pipes in the roof have broken, all that rain last night," Michael explained. "Lucky Barry gave us a reason to get out."

We all stared at previously pompous Barry; there didn't seem to be anything lucky about him at the moment. Though, except for the syringe, Barry could have been peacefully sleeping and about to bounce up with some bombastic comment about the sad state of the library.

"Nasty," Pete commented.

"Definitely not natural causes," Harriet put in helpfully.

Michael and I exchanged a glance. I often amused him and Samantha with many a work anecdote about flaky Harriet.

"Did you move anything?" Pete asked.

"No," Harriet said. "When I got here this morning, I saw Barry and ran out to Jenny."

Michael pushed at the body with the end of his pen and it

moved stiffly. "I'm no expert, but I'd say Barry's been dead for at least 12 hours."

Pete had a pen poised over his notebook. I had the surreal feeling of appearing in a crime movie. Almost on cue, he asked, "Were either of you here last night?"

Harriet and I looked at each other. "No," I replied. "The Library Board members were here around six o'clock to set this up," I waved my arm along the medical display.

"I let them in at 5:30," Harriet confirmed. "I remember because Lois Murray rang to say they were running early."

"Lois Murray," Michael repeated, writing the name on his notebook. "Who else was here?"

The Bennelong Library Board was hardly huge. Harriet wrinkled up her nose as she listed the names, extending slim fingers as she listed them off. "Simone Pollard, Sandy Griffiths, Shirley Beatie, Lois and Barry, of course," she said.

"Any of them dislike Barry?" Michael asked.

"Everyone disliked Barry," I snorted. I looked across his disfigured face and added guiltily. "Well, you know what I mean, he had a sort of pompous and annoying personality, but I can't imagine anyone doing him harm."

"Well, someone did," Pete said. "Any of those ladies likely to be having an affair with him?"

"An affair?" Harriet exclaimed with a slight snigger, no doubt stunned anyone of Barry's advanced years would consider such a thing.

"Well, none of the ladies you mentioned would be able to lift a man of Barry's size onto this table, so that suggests to me that he undressed and climbed up there himself," Michael said thoughtfully. "What happened after that is anyone's guess."

A brisk knocking sounded from the glass door around the corner.

"That'll be Jeremy," Michael said. "Let him in, Pete."

Pete Herring obediently headed to the door and retuned with a small, fidgety man clasping a leather bag.

"Now, what have we got, Michael?" Jeremy announced briskly on arrival, apparently not disposed to wasting time with greetings. The death scene before him seemed to not concern him either.

"Barry Dewey, about late fifties."

"Fifty-eight," I put in helpfully.

"Fifty-eight," Michael continued smoothly. "He was here last night with a group of women who were assembling this display. Harriet here found him about two hours ago, like this."

"In flagrante delicto," Jeremy muttered. It took a minute for the Latin translation to sink in.

"You think he died having sex on this table?" Pete asked, dark brows drawn in a heavy frown.

"Won't know for sure until I've taken some samples," the coroner said as he opened his leather bag and delved inside. "Could've had a heart attack, but I doubt it."

"Is it the syringe through his eye that gave that away?" Pete said, deadpan. Jeremy scowled. The coroner apparently had no sense of humour. Maybe that comes from too many years on the job.

"That syringe was inserted after death," Jeremy said flatly, pulling on latex gloves and snapping the end against each wrist. "Or at least when he was unconscious."

"How do you know that?" Harriet asked.

"Nothing could be inserted into the eye that accurately in a conscious person," Jeremy explained. "There's no other scratching on the face, no signs of struggle."

Jeremy examined the insides of Barry's arms and hands. "No, that syringe was thrust in afterwards, an act of anger."

"Or passion," Harriet said, eyes widening.

"Can I use your phone?" Michael asked, diverting Harriet's

fantasy. He grabbed my arm and steered Harriet and me firmly from the Middle Ages operating theatre.

"I need to speak to all of the women you mentioned." Michael told us. "I'll need to take statements. As the station's flooded we will take over the meeting room. Hope that's okay?"

The library's meeting room opened into an outdoor area on the west side of the building. Outside access made it convenient to bring in the suspects without traipsing then past the crime scene.

"Not expecting too may book borrowers today," I smiled sardonically.

"You and Harriet will need to stay also,"

"Sure," I said, handing Michael the phone receiver.

"Oh, and Jenny, you'd better put that roast back in the freezer."

Being on the Bennelong Library Board was the essence of respectability in our small town; with it came a superiority over other mere mortals, especially a middle-aged divorcee like me who had had to work full time to support myself. Because of this, it amused me to see the usually haughty board members sitting nervously on tiny chairs in the children's book section, waiting to give statements in the meeting room.

The other end of the library was now screened from view by partitions erected by the investigation people who scurried in and out carrying cameras and notebooks. More police personnel had arrived by this stage, moving with brisk importance around our usually quiet library.

Harriet, who had fully regained her sense of humour, whispered that we should take a photo for the Library Board Christmas Party. I suggested something more practical.

"Can I get you ladies a coffee to calm your nerves?" I asked.

Shirley Beatie, for one, looked as though she may pass out on the dark blue carpet. Lois' usual bright demeanour was also somewhat dimmed.

"I think that's what we all need girls," she suggested with forced cheerfulness. Shirley twisted her hands together, scrunching up her brown woollen skirt in her lap. "I can't believe someone would do this to Barry," she said. "It's terrible, just terrible." A tear glistened on her thin, papery skin.

"Such a lovely man," Sandy lamented, eyes moist. "He was so proud of our work last night."

"Are they sure it's not an accident?" Simone asked.

I thought of the glass tube protruding from Barry's eye socket. "I'd say it's pretty certain," I said calmly.

Simone nodded and hung her head again. "What do they think happened?" she asked. "Why do they suspect us?"

"Because we were the last ones with of him, of course," Lois snapped. She turned to me, "Simone left earlier and Shirley, Sandy and I left about nine o'clock. Barry insisted on staying to put the final touches on the display."

"Well, someone must have come in after we left," Sandy deduced suddenly.

"Why are we suspects?"

Michael appeared at the meeting room door. "You're not," he said soothingly. "We just need you to tell us what Barry was like last night. Did he say anything unusual? Was he worried about something? After all, you ladies were the last to see him alive."

"Except for the murderer," Shirley chipped in dramatically.

Sandy looked like she was about to faint, and I had to admit, the thought of a murderer lurking the streets of Bennelong made me feel very uneasy. First thing I was going to do after we were allowed out was fix that dicky lock on my back door.

"OK Sandy, we'll speak to you first," Michael said, holding the door open for her. Inside, Pete waited at the table, pen in hand and notebook open.

"Now, how about that coffee?" I asked the others.

I took their slight nods as a yes and took off to the staffroom, clicking on the kettle. The tiny room seemed more spacious without the conglomeration of medical supplies that had been clogging it up for the past fortnight. Used cups littered the sink, rinsed but not washed. Harriet and I were meticulous with our book shelves but lacked organisation as far as the staff room was concerned.

"Surely it can't be one of them," Harriet said quietly as she drifted though the doorway.

I was busy distributing large teaspoons of coffee in the line of cups. I hadn't asked the ladies how they took their coffee, but I figured black and strong was probably the most appropriate.

"I mean," Harriet shuddered. "Can you picture any of them even doing 'it', let alone doing it with Barry?"

"Just because they're in their seventies, it doesn't mean they've stopped functioning," I said tersely. "Besides, that's only an assumption at this stage."

Harriet looked at me sceptically. I knew she was including me in the age category of the Library Board women. I ignored her with a small shake of my head. When Harriet had initially arrived in Bennelong almost a year ago, she was totally without tact but had good qualifications. Not much had changed, though fortunately, she had mellowed somewhat in her behaviour toward our older customers.

She had her good points, one of which was sharing my opinion that Barry's hovering around bookshelves, randomly taking out books and flicking through them was distracting, and bordering on creepy! Barry had annoyed Harriet so much in that last week that she had confronted him in the third aisle; something I'd wanted to do for ages.

I linked my fingers through the steaming cups and returned to the group of shaken women. If there was a murderer among them, she was doing a good job of hiding behind a nervous exterior.

Sandy, the local butcher's wife, was quietly closing the door after just completing her statement. I offered her the first coffee. Normally outspoken and not afraid to say her piece, she looked like she needed it.

Her worried brown eyes turned to me. "I hope I said the right things," she said.

"As long as you've told the truth, that is the right thing," I murmured sympathetically.

Sandy put her hand on her face. "There's nothing to tell," she said. "Well, nothing unusual anyway. Barry was in a great mood when we left. The medical display came together so well."

Shirley lifted her head and glanced at the other end of the building, shuddering at what lay beyond the screens.

"He had some news to tell us, though," Simone put in suddenly. "Remember that? He seemed quite smug about it actually."

"News?" I pounced on her statement. "What did he say?"

"Didn't say anything to me," Shirley said. "It was probably something to do with the media release. He called in a Gazette reporter to cover the official opening tomorrow, you know."

The Bennelong Gazette was published weekly, and I could imagine them ferreting away in their tiny building at the end of the main street, hastily changing this week's headline. A murder in Bennelong was unheard of!

"Did Barry leave the same time as you?" Harriet asked from behind me.

"No, he stayed," Lois said wanly. "Simone left though."

"Kevin wanted dinner early," Simone said apologetically. "Or I would have stayed."

I nodded thoughtfully; surely Michael had already checked this detail out.

"Shirley, Sandy and I waited for it to stop raining," Lois continued. "No luck though, so we made a run for it back to the car park. We should have insisted Barry came with us."

"Perhaps he was planning to meet someone?" Shirley said suddenly.

I thought of the naked man who lay at the other end of my library. That was a foregone conclusion in my book! Then I remembered that this group of women didn't know the state Barry was in. It dawned on me: that was why the police had blocked the scene — they were trying to trip one of the women up! I glanced through the window at Michael and Pete in earnest discussion in the next room. He was so clever, my son-in-law!

We weren't permitted to touch anything, not even the sink full of dishes, so, in absence of the medical equipment, I tidied up the best I was allowed. About twenty minutes later, Michael poked his head around the corner of the doorway.

"Preliminary results indicate no signs of sexual activity, but there were drugs in Barry's system — sedatives. Seems our murderer drugged Barry, maybe persuading him to get his kit off before he passed out. Might have promised some action on the table?"

I grimaced at the thought. "Simone said he was excited. But I don't think she meant that way."

Michael chuckled. "It takes all sorts! Oh, and I was wrong, that syringe did kill him, needle went straight into the brain."

"So, any of them could have done it, strength wasn't an issue?"

"Yes, and all of them tell the same story. Got here at 5:30, left at nine, well, except for Simone. Barry stayed behind...and someone obviously met him."

"Well, he'd run out of his special tea," I commented noticing an empty packet in the nearby bin.

"What?" Michael asked quickly.

"Peppermint tea," I said, getting the pack out of the bin and showing it to Michael. "Barry loved it."

Michael snatched the pack. "This could be how the drugs were administered," he leant over the bin and started to search through it.

"What have we here," he said, coming up with a squeezed tea bag. "Have you got a bag I can put this in Jenny? I'll transfer it into an evidence bag later." I fished around in a nearby drawer for a snap lock bag.

"What? Drugs in the teabag?" I spluttered.

"No, but if something was added to the tea with the bag still in there, there could be traces of drugs in this." Michael seemed very pleased with this find. "It's a stretch but I'll get it checked — it might have been used last night. When was the library cleaned last?"

"Saturday morning," I said. "It must be from last night. Bit clumsy of the killer to leave evidence like that around"

Michael was closing the zip lock bag when Pete appeared. "Michael, we've got the press here now."

"Bennelong Gazette will be keen to have a newsworthy story for a change," I remarked.

"No, not the Gazette, the Adelaide papers — they've flown someone in and want a comment."

"There is no comment to make," Michael said testily. "Let me deal with them."

Pete and I followed Michael as far as the borrowing desk, watching as he strode out the door. Outside, the small crowd was galvanised into action by his presence, pushing towards him, one person stretching out a microphone. Michael spoke calmly, though, of course, we couldn't hear a word. Rain began to fall again, a misty film blanketing the crowd and turning the dirt and gravel path into even more of a quagmire.

Harriet sat behind her desk, but as we were forbidden to move anything, there was little she could do but sit. Shirley, Simone, Lois and Sandy sat quietly in the children's section, and though Barry had left his beloved library for the last time, the murder scene itself was still curtained off with crime scene investigators working busily behind it.

I walked along the ends of the tall book shelves and found myself turning up in the aisle where Barry usually hovered. It was strange to think he was no longer with us. I traced my fingers along the line of books; all were perfectly aligned, having been lovingly arranged by Barry and as yet not disturbed by a student's bustling fingers.

I stopped for a moment, absorbing the enormity of today's events, coincidentally pausing at the crime section. The shelves of books become unfocused as I stared into space, thinking of the last time I'd seen Barry alive. My gaze galvanised on the second shelf and suddenly, shockingly, a thought formed in my head.

Michael was shaking his wet hair when I saw him next. Despite wiping his feet outside on the mat, a line of footprints led up to where he now stood.

"That's one part of the job I hate," he said. "Dealing with the press."

"Sorry about the floor," he added.

I looked at his shoes and past his broad shoulders into the now bucketing rain. And, in an epiphany suited to an Agatha Christie novel, it suddenly all made sense.

"You should get the vacuum," I said. "But not for the reason you think."

"Huh?"

"Michael, I know who murdered Barry."

I added an extra slice of meat to Michael's plate. My daughter was back from Melbourne, but no point letting a good roast go to waste. The pork may have been a day later than planned, but it was still just as delicious.

"I should be making you dinner," Michael said. "After all, you solved the only murder in Bennelong history."

"Actually, the Library Board ladies should," quipped my beautiful daughter, Sam. "Especially as you got them off the hook!"

"You've lost your star employee, though," Michael added, loading his fork with peas and gravy.

He was right, but I didn't mind. The entire library was mine again now that Barry was dead and Harriet had been arrested for his murder.

"It was the rain that gave it away of course," I said, placing my plate on the bench. I caught the small smile that flitted between Samantha and Michael. I had been boring Michael endlessly with the details, now it was Sam's turn.

"It started raining after everyone was inside the library on Sunday evening and the floors were spotless when Harriet and I came in yesterday morning," I continued. "That meant two things — the killer hadn't been out in the rain, there was no mud anywhere—"

"And more importantly," Michael continued. "It meant that Harriet hadn't actually been inside the library this morning when she saw your mother. Turns out she had just opened the door when she told Jenny. She decided to run out and pretend she'd already seen the body."

"But wouldn't it have been better for her if you found the body together?" Sam asked.

"She panicked apparently," Michael said.

"There had been no mud vacuumed up either, so it made sense it had to be someone who had come into the library Sunday evening," I continued. "Turns out Harriet let them all in and then hid outside the meeting room until all the women had gone."

"But why?" Sam asked.

I cut enthusiastically into my roast meat. "The reason was in that blasted book section that Barry always fiddled around in. It's the true crime section. Seems our Harriet had killed some old bloke in Western Australia eight years ago and she's been on the run ever since. Nosy old Barry found her photo in a book of unsolved murders. She looked slightly different of course, but he still recognised her."

"Investigators found the book at Barry's house last night," Michael said. "The page was bookmarked and everything."

"I initially expected a photo of one of the library board women," I admitted. "To think I'd been working with a murderer for almost a year," I shuddered.

"A murderer with good references," Sam added cheerfully.

"Good forged references," Michael corrected.

"I bet Barry thought all his Christmases had come at once when Harriet offered him a quickie to forget the whole thing," Sam chuckled.

"Slimy old bastard," I said. "Still, a syringe to the eye is not a nice way to go. That image will be burned permanently into my brain."

"The syringe or Barry naked?" Sam asked with a small smile.

"Poor old Barry Dewey," Michael mused, tipping extra gravy onto his plate. "Looks like that chair position is up for grabs."

"One could say a change in the library board is *overdue*."

Sam's awful pun hung in the air as I reached for another roast potato. Health food be damned — look what my lentil salad had got me into!

PLENTY MORE FISH

WINNER: MOST SATISFYING RETRIBUTION, SCARLETT STILETTO AWARDS, 2019

Anna Tolmer's hands still shook slightly when she placed seafood dishes in front of customers, even though she had worked at Tokyo Ocean for six years. Struggling to meet the regular patrons' eyes or make small talk, Anna had at least learned to force a smile on her face. It was false but adequate, marking time before escaping back to the sanctity of the tiny kitchen. Unfortunately, this culinary peace was regularly ruined by proprietor Oshiro Togoyaki, who berated her in broken English.

"You stupid girl. You drive my customers away," he barked. "You pretty. You smile more."

Oshiro was a bad tempered, chauvinistic chef whose authentic Japanese seafood creations were his own recipes, and, consequently, he demanded suitable admiration for his efforts. Thankfully, her cantankerous boss quickly bustled out of the kitchen, his harsh words lost in the fragrant air.

"For Christ's Sake, you'd think he'd won MasterChef," Valerie scoffed derisively, dunking glassware into the kitchen sink. "The way he raves on, you would think he runs a five-star restaurant, not some shitty lunchtime café on the wharf."

Anna stifled a giggle then began stacking white crockery into the dishwasher tray. Valerie, her only other workmate, was as bold and outspoken as Anna was shy. A plump, loud-mouthed redhead twenty-five years Anna's senior, it was Valerie's exuberant personality and easy banter with customers that made the long shifts bearable.

Valerie never questioned Anna about why her promising career in vet science had led nowhere but to this menial job in waitressing. Valerie never asked why an athletic, 30-year-old blonde, who drew second glances from customers, chose to go home every evening to an apartment devoid of any company but Marty, her rescue greyhound.

Six years previously, while meandering along the wharf region of Port Adelaide, Anna had noticed a "help wanted" sign in the window of the trendy new seafood café, Tokyo Ocean. Luckily, it had been Valerie she came across when venturing inside. The older woman had sized Anna up and quickly welcomed her to the staff, easing her past the sceptical eyes of Oshiro when he strutted from the kitchen.

Valerie drew her arms from the soapy water, wiping at her broad brow with the back of one hand.

"No shit, Anna, we should quit and open our own restaurant."

"Good idea. At least we would buy our fish from the markets, not catch it ourselves," Anna muttered.

A bachelor, Oshiro spent his spare time fishing the waters around the port and using his catch in the restaurant. Anna suspected it was her knowledge of his illegal practices that stopped her employer from firing her. That and the fact that no-one else would work for him, which Valerie had assured her of early on.

"I'll get these out to Table 22," Valerie said. With carelessly dried hands, she grabbed two prepared dishes from the stainless-steel servery.

Anna had once been a regular customer at places like this. With fellow university students, she had walked confidently into restaurants and bars, ordering drinks and trying new foods. Her hair had been longer, her demeanour confident. She loved her vet science course and, back then, had no trouble looking everyone in the eye, not even the rabbits that were regularly dissected in class. How things changed.

Bitter bile rose in Anna's throat. It still happened occasionally and she cleansed it with a hastily poured drink of water. The kitchen doors swung abruptly open and Oshiro burst back in with his customary speed.

"Table three want to pay bill."

Pasting on the faux smile, Anna walked to the wooden counter at the back of the café's dining area.

The interior of Tokyo Ocean was painted stark white and decorated with stencils of black and orange koi fish swimming randomly along the walls.

"Good luck, good fortune," Oshiro explained when she began her first shift.

Anna accepted the payment, maintained a smile and waved them goodbye. They were regulars, some of the workers along the wharf's business district who escaped their offices for a quick, yet authentic taste of Asia.

As Anna closed the register drawer, Valerie bustled up alongside her with an excitement Anna recognised all too well.

"Anna, Table 14 — check him out."

Anna followed her workmate's gaze. At Table 14, against the eastern wall, sat a man aged around 35, in a business shirt and chinos. His dark head was bent forward as he studied the menu, his wallet and phone stacked neatly to one side.

"I can only see the rear view," Anna replied sarcastically.

"He's gorgeous," Valerie enthused. "Perfect for you. Go on, take his order."

Valerie had taken it upon herself to check out what she called the "talent". Though "the love of her life", Kevin, waited faithfully at home, she joked that he was easily replaceable. Valerie enjoyed scouting customers for a man for Anna, never able to understand why the willowy blonde chose to live alone with a greyhound, or why she chose to work at a dive like Tokyo Ocean with a cheapskate boss. The poor girl's last relationship ended badly apparently, or as far as Valerie could ascertain. Still, she didn't ask questions, no business of hers anyway.

Knowing Valerie would remain firmly at the counter, Anna had little choice but to take the man's order. Approaching the table, she realised that Valerie was right. He *was* gorgeous. Black hair with a slight curl, tanned skin and though she never looked directly into them, Anna glimpsed the blue-grey of his eyes.

The man tried to catch and hold her gaze but Anna was too smart for that. She took her time scribbling his order onto the notepad, an avoidance technique she had long mastered. Treacherously though, her heart raced, pulsing blood so swiftly around her body, she thought it must be audible. When he tried to speak further, she plastered on that defensive smile.

"I'll have someone bring your order out," she said quickly.

"I just don't get you Anna," Valerie said later. "He obviously wanted to know more about you. He looked hugely disappointed when I delivered the fish curry to him, I can tell you."

"Will you ever give up?" Anna asked. They were in the kitchen; the lunch rush was over and Oshiro had headed out for his customary afternoon cup of tea with the owner of Jetty Diner, a shop two doors up.

"You're wasting your life here Anna," Valerie said. "That

bloke was gorgeous and you scurried back to the kitchen like one of Oshiro's pet cockroaches. Seriously, forget your past, Anna. There's plenty more fish in the sea."

The older woman gave a dramatic sigh and stacked the last white plate on the rack.

"But, like I always say, love, it's none of my business."

Anna dreamt of him again that night — that man from her past. Charles, Charlie. It was a dream that lay dormant for months and then suddenly surfaced when she least expected it. Weird. The day had been nothing out of the ordinary, nor had her evening: home, dinner and then walking Marty on the beach as usual.

Marty, Anna's brindle greyhound, loped on ahead, his interest taken by a flock of seagulls that took flight as he got close, taunting him with their beady black eyes. Marty had come into her life unexpectedly. While walking past a rescue greyhound display in a city park four years previously, the loneliness in his sad, brown eyes had touched part of Anna's heart. Before she knew it, she was returning home with a dog. Now he was part of her daily routine: wake, work, walk the dog, repeat. It could be worse.

Anna recognised Oshiro's boat bobbing on the waves: a white, fibreglass craft with a Japanese flag flapping proudly on the bow. She lifted her chin to the wind and watched as a figure pulled in a contorting fish.

Surely Fisheries Officers knew he was regularly catching fish and illegally selling them in his restaurant?

Valerie always threatened to call the authorities and sometimes Anna was tempted to agree but, in reality, what would either of them do without a job at Tokyo Ocean? She certainly never wanted to return to those turbulent days after Charles and when she quit vet school. The dull ache of waking up to nothingness and counting the minutes until she could go back to bed, if she ever got out, was only a thought away.

When she thought she could never trust another man, Anna had met Jimmy. It was wonderful what therapy could do. Meetings with Jimmy had eased her back into life. In time, despite Charlie, her existence became a comfortable routine. No more reaching for lofty aspirations like becoming a vet, and that was perfectly fine.

Anna looked away from Oshiro's boat as Marty bounced back to her side, gazing up with his liquid brown eyes. If truth be known, they had rescued each other.

One good thing about working at Tokyo Ocean was the late start. Anna clocked on at 11:00 am, just in time for the lunchtime rush. Oshiro was preparing his catch, slicing the fillets into strips with frenetic slashes. Anna was greeted by Valerie's rolling eyes, an expression directed at Oshiro. It was the same every day.

Anna loved the monotony.

"Very busy today," Oshiro said from the corner. "Fish curry for special. I caught plenty. Cheap to make."

"I've got to hand it to Oshiro, he pulls in the customers," Anna said to Valerie as they moved out to the counter. The restaurant was filling quickly with the usual lunchtime crowd.

"Cheapskate," Valerie said. "Wish they knew he cuts corners by catching the fish himself."

"Fresh, I guess," Anna offered, picking up an order pad. "Everyone loves his fish curry."

It was a conversation they had shared a thousand times. Valerie never changed. Next, she would be telling Anna about her husband Kevin's back issues that had him laid up on Workcover. Like clockwork, Valerie chimed in.

"Kev's flat today — in a lot of pain. He thinks there's a storm coming."

Anna smiled. Early on, she had worn her hair down, a security screen against probing eyes, but Oshiro insisted it be tied back for hygiene reasons. In the end, she cut her long, golden locks into a short bob.

She received less attention after that. Perfect. Anna didn't want another Charlie in her life.

Despite telling Valerie this, the older woman remained determined to match-make Anna with any solo man that ventured into the restaurant.

"There's plenty more fish in the sea, love."

If Valerie had said that once, she'd said it a thousand times.

"Don't throw your life away over one man who treated you like shit. Good men are out there. Take my Kevin, for example." At this point Valerie would pause and release a great chuckle. "No truly, love, you *really* can take him."

Ever careful to avoid eye contact, Anna began taking lunch orders, hanging the paper slips above Oshiro's preparation bench in the kitchen. Returning to the dining room, she carried two prepared dishes — whiting and prawn dumplings. They smelt divine. Anna begrudgingly acknowledged that Oshiro was a great cook, but she never planned to tell the misogynistic prick that!

Valerie caught her eye as she passed the counter, a smug look on her face.

"He's here again," Valerie whispered fiercely.

Anna followed the direction of Valerie's eye movements. The man from yesterday was sitting at the same table. He had also ordered the same thing according to Valerie, Oshiro's famous fish curry.

Perhaps, he too, was a creature of habit?

Anna cursed herself inwardly for even considering him beyond being a customer.

"Val, seriously?"

"I'm not taking his order out, love, that's your job," Valerie said, with a teasing wink. "He's 38, works at the stockbrokers on Vincent Street. Been there a week."

Anna's mouth twitched into a small smile. Trust Valerie to wheedle that much information out of a customer.

"What, and you didn't even get his phone number?"

"Leaving that to you, love."

"Take plates, Anna. Stupid Valerie too slow," Oshiro grumbled a few minutes later as Anna stacked plates in the dishwasher. Anna said Oshiro's next words in her head, a mere second before her boss muttered them out loud.

"No-one like cold fish."

Perhaps her life was getting too predictable! Anna considered that maybe she was that cold fish that nobody liked — still, that's exactly the way she wanted it.

She had to admit though, as she plastered on her "customer smile" and placed the aromatic curry on Table 14, this diner was one attractive man. Dark hair rested on the collar of his pin-striped business shirt, which stretched across his broad shoulders. His eyes were a stormy blue and twinkled with intelligence while his plump lips curved into a smile.

"Thank you," he said. "Smells delicious."

They locked eyes for the briefest of moments before he leant over the dish to breathe the aroma.

"This won't take long," he said.

Anna froze. *What am I doing?* Blood pulsed loudly in her ears as she broke his gaze, looking instead at his phone and wallet, stacked exactly as it had been the day before. From the edge of his cuff, she could glimpse a partial tattoo. As if on cue, his sleeve pulled up slightly as he selected his fork, revealing a tiny British Bulldog. Anna hoped he didn't see her expression as she returned to the counter from where Valerie watched expectantly.

"Hot, hey?" Valerie grinned.

"He has a tattoo, a bulldog," Anna said, breathing heavily. "Charlie had a bulldog tattoo."

"So do a thousand people probably," Valerie said. "Forget that man, love. He's ruled your life for more than six years now."

Anna looked to the figure in the corner where the man was bringing large forkfuls of curry enthusiastically to his mouth.

"Maybe you're right," she admitted.

"About time," Valerie said, adding predictably. "As I've said before, there's plenty more fish in the sea."

Picking up a pile of napkins, Valerie began to fold one. Anna joined in. It was their way of looking busy while chatting, without Oshiro's gaze accusing them of laziness.

"He's not Charlie, love", Valerie said firmly, folding a napkin into a poor replica of a swan. "But he *is* Ryan Hartwell."

Anna tore her gaze from Table 14, her heart quickening.

"You asked him his name?"

"No need." Valerie took her mobile phone from her pocket and flicked the screen to Wi-Fi.

On the list of available networks were Tokyo Ocean (locked of course, Oshiro saw no need for customers to do anything but eat and then free up the table), three with generic network numbers and the last one which said *Ryan Hartwell's phone*.

"Am I a genius or what?" Valerie asked. "He's the only guy left in the cafe. That must be his name."

Anna raised her eyebrows, impressed with her friend's ingenuity.

"Very clever."

"Saw it on one of those English crime shows Kev and I watch, love. You can thank me later."

When she took Marty for a walk that evening, Ryan Hartwell was still on Anna's mind. What would Jimmy say?

She hadn't seen her therapist for over two years now, feeling they had come to a standstill. His gently probing questions and strategies no longer helped — there was no moving on from Charlie.

Finding out she could never have children had just been another blow.

Anna's head tingled with the threat of a migraine. Marty ran ahead, ever hopeful of catching one of the noisy seagulls that quickly rose into flight. Oshiro's boat was out again, the Rising Sun flapping in the strong breeze. Behind him, a bank of clouds gathered in the west. Maybe Kev's back had been right. There was a storm on the way.

As she attempted to sleep later, with Marty curled in his basket beside the bed, Anna found she couldn't close her eyes without seeing the flirtatious glance and dark hair of Ryan Hartwell. Increasing wind and the odd rattle of thunder sprang up overnight. The next morning, Anna found herself sheltering from the driving rain while attempting to open the back door of Tokyo Ocean. It was no surprise that Oshiro was even more temperamental than usual.

"Rain no good for customers," he grumbled. Judging by the aroma in the small room, Oshiro had still created his usual curry for what he had hoped would be a busy Friday.

"People still have to eat," Anna said, putting her backpack in the cupboard.

"They eat at home instead," he said sharply.

Valerie turned and predictably rolled her eyes. Anna felt instantly relaxed.

When Ryan Hartwell failed to show for his usual meal, Anna couldn't help but feel further at ease. He had intruded into her thoughts way too much. It had made her think of other things — vet school, for example. It seemed so long ago.

Oshiro's prediction proved correct, it was a slow day with

rain lashing the wharf and its shopping precinct. Valerie watched the counter while Anna filled in time by polishing cutlery in the kitchen, grateful for her boss's lack of conversation

Around 1:30 pm, Valerie came through the kitchen door.

"Anna, he's here," she whispered. "With his kids."

Anna hated the way her heart sank at that moment. *He has a family.* Typically, Valerie saw things differently.

"He has a day off. Brought his kids in," she paused and changed her tone meaningfully. "He's separated from their mother. A readymade family. It's perfect for you, Anna."

Valerie knew Anna was unable to have children and, with rose-coloured glasses firmly affixed, she considered the fact that Ryan already had children as just perfect. Never mind that Anna had barely spoken ten words to the man.

"And," Valerie smiled triumphantly. "He wants you to bring out his fish curry."

Anna peeked through the gap in the kitchen doors. Sitting predictably at Table 14 was Ryan Hartwell, casually dressed in a white t-shirt and jeans. Two dark-haired children wriggled impatiently in the seats next to him. Oshiro thrust the bowl of fish curry towards her and pointed to two smaller plates of his "specialty fish fingers".

"Hurry, stupid girl," Oshiro snapped.

Anna took a breath and delivered the meals. Ryan Hartwell smiled in appreciation, introducing his children. They were twins, named Peta and Blake. The bulldog tattoo was on full show, dancing as Ryan tucked a napkin under his daughter's chin.

"They're gorgeous kids," Anna said.

Though Anna would never experience the feeling of creating miniature versions of herself, she could appreciate the joy it brought to others.

"I'm Ryan," the man said.

Anna shook his offered hand. It was warm and smooth with perfectly clipped nails.

"Anna," she said. Her voice was clear, her smile genuine.

"It's nice to meet you."

Anna hated weekends off. The break in routine was unsettling. To thwart this, on Saturday, she decided to treat Marty with an extra-long walk along the beach. Friday's storm had churned up the sea, scattering a myriad of objects along the sand: sponges, dead marine creatures, seaweed, but mostly rubbish. As she often did, Anna carried a garbage bag to collect the trash, gathering ropes, lines and plastic, along with other random objects. Marty loped along, stopping regularly to sniff at the debris with his long nose.

Anna felt light in spirit, almost buoyant. And, though she wasn't about to tell Valerie, it was all because of the appearance of Ryan in her previously routine life.

Once home from the beach, Anna did something she hadn't done for years. She went to her bookshelf and selected a veterinary text book. After reading a couple of chapters, she was surprised and pleased how easily it all came back to her. Later, she even did some cooking, taking out her sharpest knife and chopping board, and humming while she did so.

No wonder Marty looked so confused.

Monday dawned bright, a contrast to the week before. It showed in Oshiro's mood, happy that, although unable to catch fish, his fish curry supply was still adequate.

"I almost thought he was going to crack a smile," Valerie commented. "I'm getting too old for his mood swings."

"You're not allowed to leave," Anna said chirpily.

Valerie grinned broadly.

"Well, aren't you bubbly this morning? Wonder what, or rather who, has brought that on?"

Oshiro crept up behind them, his previous cheerfulness now gone.

"I not pay you to chat. Stupid girls."

"Nope, he's still an arsehole," Valerie said once he was out of earshot.

"And how about Kev's back, Anna? Told you there was a storm coming."

Anna smiled. Some things never changed.

The café was bustling by 11:00 am. Tokyo Ocean boasted loyal customers and today was no exception. Anna was at the counter when Ryan arrived. Dressed for business, predictably, he chose Table 14, and, as usual, he ordered the fish curry. Anna knew he would — his routine was soothing. She met his eyes as she took down his order, but quickly turned away when he smiled. Force of habit.

Anna made a point of striding briskly past Oshiro, who was chatting to a customer. Her boss wore the cheesy grin that he reserved strictly for patrons — it was even falser than her own. His attitude had been totally different when informing them earlier that several fish curry dishes were prepared in advance so customers could eat and leave quickly, freeing up the tables. Typical.

Anna felt a little dazed as she entered the kitchen. She knew it was due to that smile of Ryan's. Sensing that Valerie was about to make a smart remark, Anna put up one hand in protest, colliding with an empty dinner plate on the bench and sweeping it onto the floor where it smashed into small, jagged pieces.

"Fuck!" she exclaimed.

The sound of the shattering china put Anna even more on edge. She could almost hear

Oshiro's berating voice. *Stupid girl!* Valerie leant over to help her pick up the white shards.

"Please Val, go and stall Oshiro," Anna asked, her voice shaking. "I'll clean this up before he sees it."

'Sure love,' Valerie said, giving her a comforting pat on the shoulder as she left the kitchen.

Anna continued to gather the pieces. A few minutes later she looked around the kitchen, checking she hadn't left any traces. Her heart still raced as she picked up the prepared curry dish. But, as she walked out to deliver Ryan's meal, Anna realised that, for the first time in years, her smile was genuine.

"What an exhausting morning," Valerie groaned about twenty minutes later, hurrying into the kitchen laden with dirty dishes.

Oshiro muttered something unintelligible from the corner. His customer interaction had been a complaint not a compliment which had plummeted his mood further. Anna was grateful he didn't notice a piece of his precious crockery was missing.

Anna worked in silence with Oshiro, while Valerie retreated to the front counter, settling accounts and farewelling the regulars with her usual gusto. Unexpectedly, a loud exclamation was heard from within the dining area.

"Help! Someone, please." It was Valerie.

Anna and Oshiro rushed from the kitchen. Valerie was still behind the counter but pointing shakily to the corner. Table 14.

Hunky Ryan was on the floor, his body jerking wildly.

"He's having a heart attack," someone yelled from across the room.

Anna raced over. Pushing a chair to one side, she could access his body unheeded. The man's grey-blue eyes were wide, but his lips didn't move. He was terrified. She recognised that expression well.

"Is there a doctor or nurse here?" Anna shouted. When there was no answer, she screamed, "Call an ambulance."

Anna opened Ryan's jacket and placed her hands together over his chest. Thank God her uni had insisted students have their first aid, she thought fleetingly. Even after all this time, the process came back to her quickly — 30 compressions, two breaths. She seemed to be doing it forever. It was a blur when the ambulance eventually arrived. Someone took Anna by the shoulders and moved her gently to one side. She sat heavily in a chair as they bundled Ryan onto the stretcher.

"You did everything you could. We did everything we could," an ambulance officer told her gently. "He's gone."

Valerie placed a hand on Anna's shoulder. The initial shock had worn off her workmate, who had returned to her normal, pragmatic self. She turned to Anna with pursed lips.

"Well, there's plenty more fish in the sea."

It was three weeks until Anna saw Valerie again. The former workmates arranged to meet at Jetty Cafe, two doors up from the now closed Tokyo Ocean, where Koi fish still swum sadly on the interior walls.

Anna smiled as she read the notice from the Health Commission on the familiar front door: *closed till further notice.*

Choosing a table in the afternoon sun, Valerie had lost none of her bluster or venom toward their former boss, speaking vehemently as she filled Anna's cup with green tea from a china pot.

"Oshiro was always too smart for his own good," Valerie said. "Catches his own fish then ends up poisoning someone. I couldn't wait to tell the police what he did."

And that, Anna thought, *is exactly what I had counted on.*

"Looked like the poor guy suffered a heart attack though, got to admit that." Valerie leant back and crossed her arms. "Told Kev you tried so hard with the CPR. Such a shame."

Not *that* hard, Anna thought. In fact, she had hardly compressed Ryan's chest at all. And calling for a doctor or nurse? A nice touch, she told Marty later. Risky, maybe, that someone would take over and compress Ryan's heart correctly, but Anna knew most of the customers were regulars who worked nearby and that there was not a medical person amongst them.

"It's called fugu or something," Valerie snorted, snapping a biscuit in half. "Plain old puffer fish. Can you believe it? Some Japanese delicacy old smarty pants thought he would add to the recipe. The autopsy caught Oshiro out good and proper, much as he tried to deny it."

Anna sipped her tea. It was aromatic and relaxing. Everything had been like that lately...ever since the tragic death of gorgeous Ryan Hartwell; stockbroker, family man, fish curry aficionado and creature of habit. What a respectable name for a rapist. Her rapist.

Until recently, that long ago twenty-minute act had affected every moment of her life. Yet, when Anna unexpectedly saw him again, she wasn't afraid. He had no power. All this time she had been in a prison of her own making and had let him hold the key. Him. Ryan Hartwell.

Though Anna had never known him by that name of course. Or by any name. When he snatched her off the street as she walked home through a park, a week before her fourth-year exams, he was wearing a mask. Dragging her into the bushes and forcing his weight on top of her, the only thing Anna saw as she screamed and wrestled for her life was a tattoo of a bulldog on his wrist. On the collar was a name: *Charlie*. A long-gone family pet maybe?

Charlie. Charles. That was all she ever referred to him as. To Jimmy. To Valerie. To herself. It seemed fitting somehow — Charles, like Charles Manson. An abhorrent, disgusting sociopath.

He never suspected who she was, but Anna had recognised him immediately. Besides the tattoo, it was the first words he uttered in the restaurant, mouth-watering over Oshiro's fish curry. Exactly what he said as he tore at her underwear. *This won't take long.* Anna would never forget that voice.

"Of course, Oshiro is claiming he knows the difference between a puffer fish and other fish." Valerie shrugged her shoulders. "Guess he should, he's been illegally fishing for so long."

"Stupid man," Anna said, imitating their former boss's annoying voice. And then she laughed, probably far more than was warranted. "What will you do now?" Anna asked putting down her empty cup.

It was one thing that had pricked at her conscience since dragging Valerie unwittingly into her scheme. Knocking off that plate, then asking Valerie to stall Oshiro provided Anna with the perfect chance to retrieve the special ingredients she had brought in her handbag.

As well as the rubbish on that stormy weekend, Anna had collected several puffer fish that had washed up and died on the shore. Her old vet textbooks had been so useful and left no electronic trail like there was when you surfed the net. Tetrodotoxin, deadly to dogs — and humans. A tiny pin head of the poison could kill 30 men. Yet she only needed to kill one.

Turned out she hadn't lost her dissection skills either. So simple for a trained eye to locate the deadly organs — the liver and ovaries of the poor, dead creatures. Alone in the café kitchen, she had added these delicacies to Ryan's meal while popping some of the fish's non-toxic flesh into the main pot of curry for good measure.

Ryan's assault was so brutal it had taken away Anna's chance to have children. How ironic that a reproductive organ would cause his ultimate downfall. And if that arsehole, Oshiro, ended up taking the fall, so be it. It would be manslaughter at the most. And maybe some jail time would smarten up his attitude.

Anna had always thought if she ever saw Charlie again, it would further destroy her life. However, rewardingly, she was able to destroy his instead.

And now, with Tokyo Ocean closed, it was time to move on at last. Like Valerie always said, there were plenty more fish in the sea.

And some of them could be amazingly useful.

CAT PEOPLE

To Anna@demnet.com

Subject — Animal Matters

*Morning Anna, we have another job! Feeding a couple of cats,
Monday to Wednesday next week while the owner's setting up a
cat show in Brisbane. She's some fancy cat breeder, I told her we
would love to do it! Her name is Marvelle Jones (weird I know
but then she is a cat person!) I'll meet you at Zella's at 11 and
give you the keys and the details. I'll even shout the coffee!*

Cheers, Tony

Anna groaned, annoyed her habitual checking of emails
had now ruined a sun-drenched breakfast in the courtyard. She had only switched the laptop on to view the morning's special shopping deals — a valid reason to avoid studying!

Half way through a veterinary science degree, Anna was a struggling student, who struggled even more once the morning sales arrived. Hence, the recent business brainwave that was 'Animal Matters' — if you couldn't trust a trainee veterinarian to look after your pets when you were away, who could you trust?

Anna was an intelligent woman, near the top of her class; her lecturer had only recently described Anna as an eloquent and insightful speaker. She disproved this momentarily by putting down her glass of juice with a clatter.

"Oh, shit."

Anna's flatmate's red setter, Grayson, was sprawled mop-like beneath the table and briefly raised his rusty head from his relaxed position on the pavers.

As though summoned from a nightmare, Clare appeared through the doors at that moment. She was clad in pyjamas, for which Anna was eternally thankful, having collided with her naked flatmate and her latest conquest in the hallway last Friday night.

Rings of smudged eyeliner circled Clare's brown eyes, which were closed vampire-like against the morning sun. No-one could party like a nursing student apparently, and Clare was positive proof.

When Anna replied to an ad on the uni noticeboard — *quiet nursing student needs flatmate* — it sounded perfect. She had been expecting a couple of students who were too bogged down by study to party excessively. But the truth was it was only quiet in the townhouse because Clare was never there, or rarely out of her bedroom when she was.

"Haven't you heard the one about the difference between a nurse and a ladder?" Tony has asked when Anna expressed surprise at her flatmate's habits. "Not everyone has been up a ladder!"

Clare was a dog person, Anna and Tony had decided; fun-loving, playful, although the loyalty element was definitely in question. And, as a typical dog person, she had chosen a pet based on her own appearance, with herself and Grayson sharing straggly red hair and soulful eyes. This meant that while Clare was forever late for her rent, Anna felt compelled to forgive her. At the moment though, Clare looked more like a cat searching for a nice place to curl up and sleep the day away.

"What's up?" Clare asked, collapsing into an outdoor seat and running her nails through her hair, ruffling it up into a ginger mane.

"Tony's booked us a job," Anna said. "But it's the week of my exams and it's for some crazy cat breeder."

Anna had long ago decided she was also a dog person. Sure, she was committed to fixing any animal that came into her future surgery, but cats had a smug, assured way about them that she found off putting. And two pedigree numbers were sure to up the arrogance stakes.

Clare lent her arm on the table top. "Get Tony to do it," she said simply, mumbling from somewhere beneath her pile of ginger hair. "You're partners in this thing, aren't you?"

Anna stared at the creature opposite her, startled she had made some sense. Quickly and briefly, Anna dissected her life: flatmate with revolving bedroom door, uni fees that made the national debt look small and now responsible for the over pampered pets of a woman whose name belonged to a circus magician.

Anna downed the last of her juice and wiped her mouth. She could whiz through the anatomy and physiology of bird and reptiles, but the simple things in life were sometimes difficult. But then, simpleness more or less explained why Clare had come up with the plan.

"Good idea," Anna replied.

. . .

"Bad idea," Tony said with an apologetic smile as he placed two short blacks down on the table at Zella's, a small café close to the uni. "I'm in Adelaide next week, remember?"

Tony was short and dark (like my coffee, he joked); an Australian born from Italian heritage that ran strongly through his veins. He was energetic and talkative, had a mop of dark hair and matching soulful eyes that he used to the best of his advantage.

Tony was studying commerce, a world away from animals and surgery. Tony had declared they were the perfect business pair when they met at the uni bar during orientation week in their first year; he had the business brain and she would provide hands on experience. The 'hands on experience' had connotations early on, but after three years their relationship had remained mostly uncomplicated. At least until Tony came up with his latest business plan.

"Tony, I've got exams," Anna protested.

"Think of the money," Tony replied with a winning smile. Not for the first time, Anna reflected that Tony's career choice should have been in sales.

She sipped the tiny cup of life preserving caffeine. "But why am I doing the work and we are getting the money."

Tony dabbed his mouth with a napkin. "Anna, you're the animal person and I'm better dealing with the big picture. I do my fair share. I do the advertising don't I?"

Advertising? Only if a few computer printed A4 sheets pinned up around the local area counted.

"Look," Tony conceded, brown eyes looming over the edge of his cup. "You take all the money on this one. We'll charge extra, this Marvelle woman is apparently loaded."

He tossed a set of keys on the table. Predictably, a tiny

metal cat was attached to the key ring. To that, he added a scrap of paper that held a handwritten address: *Marvelle Jones, 10 Sutton Way.*

"Another crazy cat lady!" Anna groaned, tipping her head back and talking to the skittering clouds.

"Now, Anna, we both know the world is made up of cat people and dog people," Tony said, launching into a familiar theme. "I'm a cat person, you are a dog person, we know this. You will do anything to please people. As a cat person, I am selective about who I hang out with. You should take that as a compliment."

Anna smiled wryly.

"Well, our resident dog person Clare certainly isn't selective," she agreed. "Do you know she had three different guys stay over last week?"

Tony sipped his coffee. "Is that right, Grandma?" he teased.

"I'm starting to think her nursing studies mainly involve operating procedures," Anna joked. "But I am warming to Grayson."

"You're definitely a dog person." Tony said decisively. "As for Clare, she's not too loyal and apparently not fussy."

Anna leant closer to Tony, reaching for a napkin. She could smell his musky aftershave and withdrew slightly, speaking quickly.

"This week though, I think I've bumped into the same guy twice in the hallway. Not her usual type either — bit older, slightly thinning on top. Spanish too, I actually think he said *hola.*"

"Mexican hairless?" Tony grinned. They liked to assign dog breeds to Clare's partners. "Perhaps Clare's starting to settle down?"

Anna grinned at her friend. Tony's tongue darted out to remove a line of froth on his lips, and she looked away quickly, suddenly uncomfortable. "So, getting back to Marvelle, her cats and my exams?" she said.

"Look, Anna, you know I'd stay and do it if I could, but I have to move Dad into the retirement home before next weekend. It's just a matter of throwing out a few minced chicken necks to Bob and Chopper."

Anna's raised her eyebrows, cup paused at her lips. "Bob and Chopper?

"You know how these people have pet names for their, well, for their pets." That winning smile flashed up again. Anna ignored it.

"Oh, and she wants you to give them both a quick brush each day, essential to keep their coats shiny for the Gold Coast Cat Show apparently."

"Cat people," Anna groaned.

Tony pushed out his chair and got to his feet, his cup clattered empty onto the table. "And you call yourself a vet!" he exclaimed. "See you next week."

To Anna

Subject — Crazy Cat Lady!

Hi Anna, landed safely in Adelaide. Thought I'd wish you luck for your exams. Happy studying!

Tony x
PS Don't forget Marvelle's cats, she sent me a text and said she was happy for us to name our price!

After a breakfast of home brand muesli, which Anna suspected tasted only slightly better than the cardboard box that Grayson contentedly sunk his teeth into under the dining room table, Anna found Tony's email slightly uplifting.

"Maybe I can afford some nutritional food after this week," she announced.

Clare sat across the table in her regular uniform of pyjamas. About an hour earlier, as she lay in bed contemplating the day, Anna had heard the pitter patter of feet and quiet unlatching of the front door.

"Who was the early riser?" Anna asked. They had been flatmates for nearly two months now, and she had quickly learned Clare loved sharing her conquests.

"Patrick," Clare smiled mischievously. "You know? The one with the accent?"

"The Spanish accent? And his name's Patrick?"

"His mother is Irish apparently," Clare said. "Patrick owns his own marketing business. He had an early flight to Sydney."

Anna cocked her head to one side as she munched on indigestible flakes. "That's the most I've ever heard you talk about one of your ... " she paused to tactfully select the right word. "Friends."

But the inference, like most things, was lost on Clare. "It's the most I've wanted to know about one," Clare said thoughtfully, selecting a brown bowl from the sink where it had air dried the night before. "I really think Patrick might make me change my ways."

Clare leant across and grabbed the box of muesli. "May I?" she asked. "I'm skint for the week."

"Rent's due Friday," Anna reminded her. As far as the cereal went, she was welcome to it.

Clare flashed one of her feline smiles. "It's all good, Patrick's spotting me a loan when he gets back."

Anna sighed and pushed the tasteless cereal across the table. "And I have to go out and feed cats to make my half of the rent!"

The nuts and oat flakes tinkled into Clare's bowl. "You love it," she said brightly, pushing a stray lock of hair behind one ear. "You're becoming a vet after all."

Anna reached out with her foot and ruffled the rusty fur under Grayson's ear where he relaxed on the carpet. "It's not that I don't like cats, but I'm a dog person," she attempted to explain, but it was lost on Clare. Tony would understand of course, but he was lugging recliners into the Shady Rest Retirement Village or some such place.

"I'm not fussy," Clare mused.

Anna controlled herself enough not to reply. "Well, better go give Bob and Chopper their first load of minced chicken for the day then it's off to the last tutorial before tomorrow's exam."

"Bob and Chopper?" Clare giggled.

"Don't ask."

With the GPS instructing her in its weird electronic voice, Anna turned her tiny blue car into Sutton Way. It was only a few suburbs from their unit and conveniently en route to the uni. The street was part of one of those suburbs that had sprung up post-war where original houses were easy to pick; basic red brick homes with near identical squares of lawn edging low, white-washed front fences. Even many gardens were similar with rows of well-controlled rose bushes, pruned for the approaching spring.

There were a few exceptions of course; some tended their gardens better than others. It usually followed that the unkempt ones were rental homes, with gardens left overgrown and rambling. There was a deli to the right as Anna drove along, *Four Star Takeaway*, optimistically named, going off of the grimy window and its flaking paint.

Almost at the end of Sutton Way, Anna saw a sign jutting up from an immaculate lawn, indicating she was now arriving at the "House of Marvelle" as Tony had joked. According to a quick glance at the red and black sign, she was not only a well-known cat breeder, Marvelle's felines had also won several national championships.

Anna parked out front, grateful at least that she didn't have to discuss the endearing qualities of the kitties with their adoring owner. Despite Marvelle's questionable sanity, Anna had to admit that the garden was immaculate, in stark contrast to the monstrosity which was the house opposite.

Across the road, two cars blocked the driveway, hoisted up onto cement blocks. Judging by the framework of weeds, the wrecks hadn't been moved anywhere for a very long time. An impassable knot of roses that edged the front boundary had grown into a matted, thorny hedge, poised to engulf the dilapidated vehicles at any time. Anna shook her head angrily. People like that gave renters like herself a bad name!

With the jingling cat charm key, Anna let herself in the front door, peeking in nervously. It was weird to be inside someone else's house, especially one as cutesy pie as Marvelle's. The darkened hallway was papered with broad lemon stripes, plastic flowers stood silently in vases and, as she and Tony had anticipated when she dropped the annoying man at the airport, there was a requisite collection of feline figurines. Cat people were so predictable!

In the back sunroom, to the left of the floral lounge, a fridge whirred quietly as it cooled containers of gelatinous chicken neck, minced into a pink and white conglomeration. Luckily, three years of dissection, blood and guts had rendered Anna's stomach invincible to most things. She grabbed a container of the minced goo and went to the back yard.

In the corner were two cages, side by side and containing two large, pacing cats. No doubt this was the beloved Chopper and Bob who yowled at the indignity of their containment and apparent starvation. They considered Anna briefly, smug expressions plastered on their furry faces. Anna knew what this expression meant — *About time you turned up!*

Anna opened the cage door slightly and slid inside, well aware of how slippery cats could be. Today though, the chilled minced chicken necks had Bob and Chopper's attention more than the possibility of freedom.

"There you go guys," Anna said, pulling what remained of the sticky mess from her fingers, flicking a wad of chicken skin on the back of one of the animals into the process. Probably not something they gave marks for at the upcoming cat show.

Fortunately, two brushes hung nearby and, as per instruction, Anna ran the bristles through their fur, removing the piece of unfortunate poultry. For a moment she sat and watched the cats gorge themselves on the food; pedigree or not, all cats were gutses. And then, when she could put it off no longer, it was time for her latest class in the anatomy of vertebrates.

"Break a leg Anna," she said aloud, carefully relatching the cages. "Leg, anatomy, get it?" she asked the cats, who chose to ignore her now she had served her purpose.

Bob and Chopper were both cleaning their paws like a pair of furry bookends. Typical! She could picture Tony's brown eyes screwing up at her lame humour. Maybe she missed him after all.

That evening, Anna sat amongst open textbooks on the lounge. Grayson took up the seat beside her, his rusty head resting on a tome of physiology. Initially, Anna had insisted Grayson stay outside, but his big brown eyes and a flick of his tail had seen that last about three weeks. Somehow in the last four weeks, he had weaselled his way onto the lounge. And, as she told Tony, Grayson was better company than Clare anyway, and probably twice as intelligent.

They had sat in companionable silence for about an hour, interrupted only by the turning of pages, when the door opened and in came Clare and Patrick.

Clare had one arm draped around his neck and Anna was fairly sure Patrick's hand was travelling over Clare's rear end when they saw her sitting on the lounge and abruptly stopped their impromptu body searches.

"Anna," Clare exclaimed.

"Hi Clare." Anna forced a smile. "Patrick," she nodded.

Patrick looked surprised that Anna remembered his name. Damn my photographic memory, she thought, it always made men wary.

It was the first time Anna had really seen Patrick, other than fleeting glances in the dull hallway. He was older than Clare's usual conquests as she had suspected and more than slightly balding. Mature age student? Then Anna remembered Clare had said he had his own business. Anna knew better than to ask details because she doubted Patrick would be around for long.

Still, she took in the slightly podgy face and tanned complexion, mentally noting details to discuss with Tony once he returned from Adelaide. Patrick's hair was dark, and though she doubted it was natural, his slight Spanish accent seemed genuine enough.

"I thought you had a business trip?"

"Not until tomorrow," Patrick replied with what Anna suspected was an emphasised roll of his r's.

"You wouldn't believe Patrick has lived in Australia since

he was eleven, would you?" Clare gushed. "He sounds straight from the streets of Madrid,"

Well, that probably covers quite a few years, Anna thought sarcastically. Still, she didn't know whether to be more impressed that Clare knew Madrid was in Spain or the fact that Patrick managed to control the lust in his eyes as Clare's breasts threatened to break free of her singlet top.

"Patrick's helping me study," she giggled. "Anatomy."

Anna smiled weakly. "Well, I'm about to go out and feed the cats again," she said. "I'll be about half an hour," she added pointedly.

Down the hallway, Clare's door clinked shut. Grayson looked at her soulfully as Anna grabbed her keys and headed for the door

"I'll try to be quick," she assured him.

To: *Anna*

Subject — *Missing Me?*

From: *Tony*

Hi Anna (Dog Person), want the good news or the bad news? Good news — we don't have to feed Marvelle's cats all week. She has decided to stay up in Brisbane to prepare for the cat show and wants Bob and Chopper air freighted up there to prepare. Bad news — she wants us to do it! More later.

Tony (Cat Person) x

Anna grimaced at her keyboard. The supposed relaxing atmosphere of the courtyard was not doing its job of late.

The nerve of him! WE have to feed the cats, yeah right!

To top it off, he thought a kiss at the end of the email would get him off the hook.

Doesn't he think I've got enough to do? I've got two exams today and I want to cram until at least ten-thirty. Now I don't only have to feed the stupid cats, I've got to prepare them to go on holiday.

Clare was being annoyingly smug after her noisy night with Patrick. "You know, I think you complain about Tony so much because you secretly have the hots for him."

"That's ridiculous," Anna said, though she could feel her cheeks flaming. "He is infuriating and inconsiderate."

"Look," Clare said calmly. "Why don't I feed the cats for you today?"

Anna hoped her look of amazement wasn't too obvious. "Would you really do that?"

"Sure, I've got nothing planned. Patrick's away ... "

"What about study though? You've got exams as well."

Clare dismissed that with a flick of one hand before pointedly extending her ring finger. "That's fine, mine's only two hours. Anyway, I don't think I'll need to study much longer. I think Patrick's bringing me something important back from Sydney."

"Your rent money?" Anna asked pointedly.

"I think he's the real thing Anna. I think we could spend our lives together."

"You've only known him four weeks," Anna reminded her, but there was no point going on. Clare's eyes had glazed over, which generally meant her brain was in neutral.

"Look Clare, if you could feed the cats that would be great," Anna said, delving around in her hand bag.

"Here's the keys to the front door and the address. There's chicken necks in the fridge in the back room, and you'll need to check the water and give them a brush."

Clare studied the card. "Don't stress Anna, I won't kill Marvelle's prize winning pedigrees, you can count on me!"

While the words of her flatmate didn't fill her with confidence, Anna had little choice. She climbed in her car and followed Clare down the road. At least with Sutton Avenue on the way to the uni, she could be sure Clare turned down the right road.

With a sigh of relief, she returned her flatmate's wave as Clare turned her mini into Sutton Avenue. Anna cleared her mind of cats and ran through the diseases and disorders of cows. She manoeuvred her car into the car park and tried to focus her mind when a text beeped through on her phone.

Hey Anna, Marvelle want the cats at the airport at lunchtime Wednesday (tomorrow!) There are two travel crates in the back shed. There's a section for despatching animals in the freight department. Then you can pick me up at 1pm at gate 3 — Dad's all shifted in so I'm heading back early. As a loyal dog person, I know you'll do this! Tony x

Anna snapped her phone shut. Another smooth over kiss! How could Clare even imagine she found the man attractive? She would deal with Tony later.

While it was no surprise to spot the same pot of soup that had been boiling away in the cafeteria for four days now, it was a surprise to Anna to see Clare dipping into a bowl of it when she came out of her first four-hour exam. Of course, Clare also had an exam, it's just that with the morning's statement, she wasn't sure if her flatmate was going to bother with the whole thing.

Anna slid into a chair opposite Clare and was about to comment on the soup when Clare brushed back her red hair and pushed it behind one ear. Across one cheek a thin red line arched angrily toward her nose. Her eyes were red and watery.

"Clare," Anna exclaimed "What happened to your face?"

"Don't think I'm a cat person either, Anna,"

"Have you been crying?"

Clare wiped her eyes. "Allergy," she explained.

Anna dipped her brows doubtfully; there was an awful lot of water coming out of Clare's big brown eyes and no longer a cat to be seen.

"I put those revolting chicken necks in their bowl and when I knelt down to check the water, I trod on one of the cat's tails."

Clare paused to point at the gash across her skin. "The bloody thing jumped up and scratched me. You didn't tell me they were so highly strung."

Speaking of highly strung ...

"Well, they are pedigree," Anna offered weakly. "Have you put some antiseptic on it?"

"No time, I have an exam, don't I?"

Clare seemed genuinely shaken.

"Look, I'll do the cats tonight," Anna said. "Tony messaged me to say they have to get freighted up to Brisbane tomorrow, so I'll have to find the crates and everything anyway."

"Typical male," Clare spat. "Everything is left up to you. They can't be trusted."

"I don't think Tony meant—" Anna started, before realising she was defending Tony, which would only add fuel to the fire of Clare's ridiculous suspicions. Though, going on her messed up appearance that was furthest from her mind right now.

Something niggled at the edge of Anna's mind, but the

angry scratch across Clare's face focused her attention on her distressed flat mate.

"You know, cat claws are really unhygienic," Anna said. "You really should put some antiseptic on that."

"Later," Clare said with a sniffle, consulting her watch. "Right now, I have an exam."

That afternoon, buoyed by the relief of ticking off the latest step on her seemingly endless journey to become a veterinarian, Anna once again parked her car outside the home of Marvelle Jones, pedigree cat breeder, at the end of Sutton Street.

She passed through the hallway and even touched a tacky figurine of a white Persian with tenderness. Such was her good mood, the cats' sullen faces and demanding yowls couldn't even put a damper on it. She located the two blue air freight cages and decided to place them by the cats' bowls so the stress of the next day's exams wouldn't make her forget to deliver Bob and Chopper to the airport.

Strangely, it appeared the pack of chicken necks were not much smaller than the day before. Bob and Chopper stretched their wiry bodies up to the mesh, their bowls were licked clean, and they paced unhappily.

"You guys can sure eat," Anna said, dipping into the gelatinous bag of poultry necks.

It was a juggle with the bag and the air freight basket. Anna manoeuvred her fingers beneath the cage lock and it sprung open with more force than intended. Chopper saw his chance for freedom and streaked through the open space, bounding on to the grass and stopping to sniff a stray leaf.

Anna let out an expletive and dropped the cage and bag of

meat, chicken necks oozing onto the lawn. Her prior low stress levels were skyrocketing.

"Chopper, come here, mate," she cajoled. "Here puss," she extended out a pale offering of chicken neck. "Look what I've got."

But Chopper was more interested in his sudden discovery of freedom. He bounded down the side of the house and out onto the road. Anna chased after him, willing a car not to be speeding down the street.

Out on the bitumen, Chopper walked in that annoyingly quick pace cats have mastered; not speedy enough to appear hurried but not slow enough to catch either.

Chopper ducked into the overgrown rose bramble of the house opposite. The place looked like it belonged to a den of bikie drug users, but Anna preferred to take her chance with them rather than Marvelle, the crazy cat lady.

Squeezing between the rust bucket of a car and the thorny hedge, Anna spotted Bob sitting complacently next to a pile of rubbish on the overgrown front lawn. An abandoned plastic child's car was resting in the garden, which made Anna feel more comfortable. At least if the bikie drug users had children, they might be more accepting of her traipsing after some stupid cat in their front yard.

But on closer inspection, the pile of rubbish was not quite as it appeared — it was the crumpled body of a man: balding, middle aged, with a kitchen knife protruding from his chest. It was Patrick, the Irish Spaniard.

The police were surprisingly quick to respond. Anna got Chopper back in his cage, threw out a few chicken necks and waited outside Marvelle's house for the cavalry to arrive. Exams, cats freighted to Brisbane, even Tony was forgotten in the myriad of questions. Why was she there? How did she find the body? Did she know the deceased?

Anna answered the questions as best she could, but that thing that had niggled her since lunch time...she had to mention it. In the end, she told the police officer everything she knew, and everything she suspected.

At noon the next day, Anna packed Bob and Chopper into their cages, ignored their protests and drove them to the airport. She picked up Tony and brought him back to the blessedly quiet flat. Grayson lifted his rusty head from his paws and looked at them happily as they came through the door.

"So, what's been happening?" Tony asked. He looked fresh, despite his flight from the west, sexy even, Anna dared to think.

Tony looked around the apartment, and she knew he expected to see Clare appear from her busy bedroom.

Anna had managed to contain herself since the airport.

"Not much. Exams, feeding stupid cats, murder ... "

For once, Tony was speechless as Anna told Tony the events of the past few days and the reason why the flat was so quiet. Clare had been arrested on suspicion of murdering her Spanish lover!

"But, what tipped you off? Tony asked eventually.

Anna enjoyed the way Tony followed her to the courtyard, desperate to know what was going on. Grayson followed close behind as Anna clicked onto the emails on her open laptop.

To: Anna and Tony

Subject — Animal Matters

From: Marvelle

Subject: My babies

Hi Anna and Tony, thank you so much for looking after Bob and Chopper. They were so excited when they arrived in Brisbane and I'm sure they'll win best in show! Thanks again,

Marvelle Jones

"I still don't get it," Tony said.

"Marvelle is a pedigree cat breeder, right?" Anna began with a mysterious smile.

Tony nodded.

"That was no cat scratch on Clare's face, it was a scratch from the rose bushes across the road where Patrick lived ... with his wife and three children! Clare told me she fed the cats, but the poor things were starving,"

Anna paused, suddenly aware how close Tony stood as they looked down at the laptop. She plunged ahead with her story.

"The clincher was that she told me she stepped on one of the cat's tails which is why it scratched her. That's when I knew she hadn't even been in Marvelle's house. Turned out, she pulled up, spotted Patrick and, well, you know the rest. But it was Clare saying she had trod on Bob's tail that really gave it away."

"Why?" Tony's voice appeared to have grown husky in his days away. Anna wondered why she didn't rent a place on her own years ago.

"Work it our for yourself," she said, clicking a key on the computer before turning to find her breath against his cheek.

In the attachment Marvelle had sent, Tony and Anna at last saw a photo of their temporary employer. There was the crazy cat lady, red hair and orange clothes, as glaringly clashing as one would expect, standing at her booth for the upcoming show. In front of Marvelle, Majestic Duke Robert, aka Bob, seemed to have a smile on his inscrutable tawny face as she stroked his back.

But most importantly, in the background, was the sign, and Anna placed a finger on one very important word. "Marvelle Jones, *Manx* cat breeder"

"Cat people!" Anna said softly.

"Cat people," Tony echoed and he leant in close.

REVENGE TAKES THE CAKE

'WINNER: BODY IN THE LIBRARY, SCARLETT STILETTO AWARDS, 2020

B arbra Foster's kitchen dresser was lined with ribbons blue.

When it came to cooking contests, she knew them through and through.

Jams, preserves and chutneys, bread and spongy cake,

the entire town of Balsa said there was nothing she couldn't bake.

"I get it from my mother," said Barbra, rosy cheeked.

"Such a shame she died at 55, before she really peaked!"

Twenty years more on from Mum now, Barb knew what was the go,

and how to win (yes, yet again) the Balsa Rural Show.

With such a reputation of perfect scones and pie, of course the local paper sent a writer by.

Barbra plastered on a smile, her ample chest puffed out,

serving up a fluffy cake so the girl could have no doubt
that the legend local baker, such a modest, humble lass,
could put her cooking where her mouth was (to brag would
just be crass).

Choccy lipped and stomach full, the journo left with cheer,
assuring Barb she'd win again — her 22nd year.
"I'm still not happy with who's the judge," said Barb, her
grey head shaking,
she'd telephoned her good friend Peg, in a rare break from
the baking.

"I've never liked old Wally Twiss; he smokes and drinks flat
beer.
So, I'm planning to retire once I win the show this year."
"And he doesn't like me either, that pompous, balding
man!"
"Win him over with your pies," said Peg, "You know you
surely can!"

So, affixing her pink apron, flour dusted on her hands,
Barb attempted cockles and tampered with friands.
In the middle of this frenzy, the flour bag ran dry.
With only one more day to go, she thought she may
just cry!

Ducking in the aisle of the Balsa General Store,
Barb sought out the flour and found what she'd come for.
But as she clasped the packet and placed it in her trolley,

a voice came from the aisle next door — no mistaking it was Wally.

"Barb Foster's had her way too long, she dominates the Show.
    Its time another won the prize, old Barbra has to go."
    Next voice was Joycie Smithers, all coy as it filtered through.
    "Oh Wal, you are a joker, did you know I'm cooking too?"

That horrid, balding little man, Wally bloody Twiss,
    Barb hadn't liked him anyway and now he's spouting this!
    Barb jammed her shopping in her bag, leaving them behind,
    but passing by a bag of nuts, a spark flashed in her mind.

Come Balsa Show Day, Barb stacked the cakes, she really had to dash.
    But not before she cleared a space for her expected new blue sash.
    In the wooden hall, Barb's fluffy cake was the last one in the row!
    Joyce smiled from across the room, her pearly teeth on show.

And quick to take her chance, as Joycie chatted to her niece,
    Barb stuck a nib of peanut in Joyce's sliced off taster piece.
    Wal was always on about his allergy, as if it really mattered...

More important than his whining, Barb sniffed, is that my reputation is unshattered.

She met Wally's smarmy smile with a smug one of her choice,
waiting for his reaction when he took some cake from Joyce.
It happened fairly quickly; Barb quite sure he overreacted.
He sputtered, fell, then turned quite blue, his pupils were contracted.

Apparently, it was touch and go, Barb later heard from Peg.
"Don't be daft," Barb chuckled. "Those doctors love to pull your leg."
She'd rearranged her ribbons, spread them out to hide the space.
And in spite of all the nonsense, a broad smile stretched Barb's face.

While the end of Balsa cooking comps was one thing this drama cost.
Although she may not have won, Barb also hadn't lost!

LOOSE ENDS

'The sound of a kiss is not so loud as that of a cannon, but its echo lasts a great deal longer.'

— OLIVER WENDELL HOLMES

I t was today.
   Meg Tudor turned the well-handled invitation in her hands, breath catching sharply in her throat. She scanned the words for the hundredth time.

Class Reunion!
   You are invited to re-join the 1991 class of Bells Bay High.
   Party at Echo Beach, just like we used to!

. . .

To an outsider of the class of '91, the letter signified nothing more than a corny get together at a local beach that happened to share its name with a popular song from the '80s. That old Martha and the Muffins tune had jingled regularly through Meg's head lately, recalling the comparatively carefree days of Year 12.

Hard to believe 30 years had flown by. Back then, any dream seemed attainable. What a shame ambitions changed when confronted with the real world.

Not that things had turned out too badly for Meg. Working in the local pharmacy, followed by quiet nights by the television, was nothing to be ashamed of. So, she hadn't left the town in which she was educated or embarked on that big career in marketing? Still, Meg's life generally satisfied her. At least until recent events forced her to reassess.

Meg slipped the invitation into the bin. The clock showed quarter past eleven: time to head to the beach. She grabbed the car keys from the table. The key ring was a tiny surfboard; a sentimental concession to her youth. She felt silly when she bought it, served by a stick thin, bored teenager. Enclosing it in her hand, Meg strode purposefully to the door. Time to get this reunion out of the way and move onto the more enjoyable events planned for later in the afternoon.

It was a short drive to the windswept beach. Meg parked her car at the eastern end, intending the brisk ten-minute walk to the location of the reunion to clear her head.

The car park was empty. It wasn't one of those neat, newly-established areas, smartly edged with painted white posts, rather, it was the same dusty place where she and her friends once parked their Datsun's and Torana's. The trees were bigger now of course, but as Meg's shoulder brushed against a shrub, a familiar scent of eucalyptus wafted from the bruised leaves.

A few winding metres through the trees to the cliff top and

Meg felt the breeze viciously toss her recently coloured hair. Echo Beach was a wild, savage edge of the ocean, but the class of 1991 had enjoyed good times on this beach.

Meg and Cate adjusted their bikinis and gazed from the bushes onto the shore. Several people splashed in the water below: "Jack's here," Cate said.

Meg had noticed that, of course. He stood waist deep in the ocean; wet, tanned skin shimmering in the sun. Gail Dennis frolicked next to him, squealing as he flicked water at her.

"She's such a bitch," Cate said.

Meg didn't reply, not wanting to acknowledge the knot in her stomach that appeared at Jack's simple flirtatious action. Instead, she stared out to the endless blue horizon.

Standing in that same place now, the beach was deserted. The lashing waves and undertow, once ignored by youthful ambivalence, had seen the beach become less popular in recent years. About a kilometre to the west, the sand stopped abruptly, and the shore became littered with huge boulders from the crumbling cliff face. Memories of Meg's time in high school lived in those shadows, the place of choice for weekend parties.

Woolen jumper pulled close; Meg leant against a cold, rough rock. Jack stood nearby, framed by a deep, angry, green ocean and crowned by an inky sky that twinkled with stars. He threw his head back often and swigged from a beer. The fire spat occasionally, sending out a short-lived display of sparks and casting an orange glow over the gathered crowd — Meg's classmates, who had told a variety of excuses to cover their absence from home.

"Nice night."

Ben's voice surprised her. He was staring, a long hank of sandy hair brushed across startling emerald eyes.

"I guess," Meg said.

Ben was new in town. He lurked in the background of her English lessons and had an annoying habit of whistling in class.

She tried to ignore him. In the light of the fire, Jack smiled smugly before throwing the empty bottle into the fire where it smashed into a thousand pieces.

In 1991, they shimmied down the cliff, bent legged and leaning back for balance, careful not to flick grey dirt onto their reef-oiled legs. Today, Meg was pleased to use the recently installed steps. While many local residents considered it a waste of money at a beach few people visited, Meg was thankful for every plank.

The angle of the cliff at the far end of the beach swallowed up the sunlight, leaving an arc of cooling shade. It was impossible to see if anyone else had already arrived for the reunion. Flicking off her sandals, Meg dug her bare toes into the cool sand. There was no point delaying things any longer, but she was reluctant to move from the quiet safety of her position.

Would Jack have read the invitation? Would he be there waiting amongst the jagged rocks?

Gail and Jack stood close to each other. Meg burned inside. Gail had it all. Blue eyes, throaty laugh, perfect teeth. Yet, Meg would give up everything for Jack — even the one thing not many of her classmates still had to offer.

"What do you see in him?"

It was Ben again, creeping up out of the shadows as he had the previous weekend.

"What are you talking about?"

Ben laughed. It was a low, surprisingly warm sound.

"Oh, come on, I mean Jack. Can't you see he's only interested in himself?"

"What would you know?" Meg snapped.

Ben looked at her so intently, Meg was forced to look away.

"More than you think," he said. "I watch people, observe things."

"Some sort of psychiatrist, are you?" she retorted smartly.

"One day," Ben said.

Meg stared at him, taking in the slightly crooked nose and intense green eyes.

"Hey Meg." It was Jack's voice floating across the fire. "Want a wine?"

Meg nodded. Why not? She'd show Ben and his smart comments.

Gail offered her a plastic cup. "Scull it down," she encouraged.

Meg tipped the cup up and instantly her mouth was on fire. With a strangled splutter, she spat the contents into the sand, coughing and gasping, eyes running and face turning red. Even in her limited experience, Meg knew enough to recognise straight vodka.

"Sorry Meg," Gail said, her voice punctuated with laughter, "I must have got the wrong bottle."

Jack was doubled over; every guffaw was like a stab to her heart.

By the time Meg had recovered, Ben was gone.

Stopping to stretch, Meg turned for a moment, facing the way she had come. Every one of her footprints had been washed away as though they never existed.

She viewed the rocks of Echo Beach with real trepidation. What had happened to the dreams of all her classmates: self-obsessed Gail who planned to be a flight attendant, Cate, who dreamed about getting into fashion?

Strange how people forced together at school drifted slowly apart in the end, Meg mused. Each of them had followed their own journey in life, with some not taking the road they had expected. Look at her own dreams! How often things didn't work out as planned.

"I thought you were studying to be a psychiatrist? What's with English class?"

Ben looked up, holding one finger on the text to mark his place.

"Well, you're in it."

Meg shifted uncomfortably.

"Plus, I like Shakespeare," Ben said easily.

Not a cool thing to say, but that didn't seem to bother Ben.

"We should get together and study," Ben suggested. "Tonight?"

Meg shrugged. "Sure. Hey, how come you don't do that annoying whistling anymore?"

Ben grinned. "I don't have to, you've finally noticed me."

That afternoon, Meg walked with Ben to 'The Squatter's Arms', the hotel his parents owned.

In the empty pub dining room, they spread schoolbooks over brown Laminex tables. Meg marveled at the easy way Ben slipped his hand over hers and his green eyes sparkled at her embarrassment.

. . .

Bare feet splashing through the shallow water, Meg approached the shadowy rocks of the point. Thoughts of Ben added speed to her steps. And memories of Jack. Just like 30 years before, they fought for her headspace. Jack and that broad, cheeky smile that seemed made just for her.

Back in 1991, as third term progressed, traipsing after Jack and his football matches became less important. Instead, she had lay on her towel on this very beach, studying chemistry while Ben whirled and dipped through the waves on his board. When he came in, he leant across her body and kissed Meg full on the mouth, seawater dripping onto her skin and running in cool rivulets down her neck.

Meg came across Jack one afternoon between classes, leaning casually on the science lab wall.

"Hey Meg, haven't seen you around much."

"Jack, I see you every day."

He flashed his killer smile but contempt laced his voice. "I mean really seen you — down at Echo Beach. Too busy hanging with the pub rat?"

"Shove it Jack," Meg flared.

"Cool down," Jack grinned. "We just miss you round the fire that's all." He paused for maximum effect. "Well, I do."

In spite of herself, Meg blushed.

"You know Gail and I have broken up?"

Meg nodded.

He touched her shoulder and hoisted himself from the walk, walking nonchalantly away.

"Just thought you might be interested that's all."

Ben appeared at the corner of the building. "What was that about?" he asked.

"Nothing," Meg said quickly.

There was no suspicion in his voice. Ben didn't play games. His arm draped over her skin with warmth and protection, not possession.

She reached up to kiss him.

"What was that for?"

"I think I love you."

Ben smiled in that gorgeous, funny way.

"Well, it's about time," he said.

Things moved fast after that. Was it really thirty years since that first innocent flush of love? The reunion had made her nervy lately, making the passage of time painfully apparent.

Rapidly closing the distance, Meg could see someone sitting on a rock. Although she spent Year 12 with 42 other people, Meg had no doubt who it was.

Ben and Meg had walked together from school as usual. The year was fast coming to an end with every conversation revolving around future plans.

Ben's mother met them at the hotel door.

"No studying in here today, we've had a busload of tourists turn up. You'll have to go into the house."

"I've got a better idea," Ben grinned once they were alone.

He reached across the bar and grabbed a key from the long row of hangers.

"How about room three, Madam?"

Ben's voice was low and clear, as was the meaning of his words.

Later, they lay curled into each other on the striped quilt cover. Macbeth was long forgotten. In fact, the book was not even opened on the side table.

. . .

Tears stung Meg's eyes at the rawness of the memory. Had attending this reunion been a good idea after all? She flicked away the tears with one finger and picked up pace, closing the final fifty metres to the end of Echo Beach.

The last exam was over. The bonfire was well ablaze at Echo Beach, and sounds of laughter floated on the cool smoky air. Meg scanned the faces for Ben.

"He's not here."

Jack stepped out of the crowd, beer in hand. Meg ignored the arrogant jut of his chin and his cold and slightly drunken gaze.

"He had to work at the pub," Cate said. "His Dad picked him up. He wasn't happy."

Meg frowned.

"Don't look so stressed," Jack said with an easy smile.

"Yeah, celebrate with us," Cate said, linking her arm through Meg's.

Someone passed her a bottle and Meg took a swig. They were right, Ben would want her to celebrate.

The endless wine was cool on her throat. Soon, Meg felt lightheaded and relaxed, laughing loudly when someone threw a physics text book in the fire.

Later, Cate appeared at her elbow saying something about leaving. Her image was blurred through the smoke, her voice lost in the waves.

"But it's party time Cate, we're finally out of school, free..."

"Well, I'm going home." Cate said.

From somewhere came another wine cooler, and another...

Eventually Meg noticed the fire had lost its warmth. She saw Jack's angled face and realized they were the only two left. His eyes were hungry and wild as he came toward her. Meg stumbled backwards into one of the boulders of Echo Beach.

Jack loomed dangerously close. Meg knew she could have what she had always wanted now. In an instant his mouth was on hers.

The stocky figure reclining against the rock turned as she approached. It was exactly who Meg expected to see. Thirty years hadn't fully eroded his sharp profile. Even though his skin sagged slightly and his eyes were creased, it was obvious he had once been a very attractive man. His hair was cropped short and he wore jeans and a white t-shirt that skimmed the curves of a slight paunch.

"Jack."

Behind Jack, another set of newly constructed steps wound their way to the cliff-top. He stood up, abruptly blocking the view. She'd forgotten how tall he was.

A smile spread over his face, that same old smile that had once been her master. No doubt it had been put to good use over the years.

"Meg." He leaned over and gave her a hug, lips brushing her skin.

"It's been a while," she said. She was pleased to see he was alone.

"Sure has. You look great." He glanced around the empty beach. "Seems we're the first ones here."

Meg sat her sandals on the nearby rock and smiled. "Looks like it."

He was staring at her, but his eyes had long lost all their power.

"So, what do you do with yourself? Teaching, wasn't it?"

"Marketing," Meg said tightly. "That didn't quite go as planned. How about you? Married?"

That grin again. "Twice. Neither time too successfully. You?"

"No, that never quite happened either. I work at the pharmacy in Bells Bay."

Jack nodded. He hadn't shaved for a day or two, she noticed, and the regrowth was grey. The spiky hair on his head retained much of its blondeness though, whether natural or otherwise.

"I'm in Perth now, I run my own export consultancy business called JackEx. You might have heard of it."

Meg shook her head. Could he tell she was lying? That she knew every detail of his life? No surprise he'd been so successful in everything. Except relationships.

"We had some great times here," Jack said.

"Some," Meg said crisply, treacherous tears springing to her eyes.

Jack didn't notice. "Wonder what the other guys turned out like? You're still looking pretty good Meg."

She hadn't imagined she'd feel so uneasy being alone with him again.

"It's hot down here," Meg said, running one agitated hand through her hair. "Want to wait up the top of the steps in the breeze?"

His smug grin told Meg that Jack was well aware of the effect he was having on her. It was true, she felt almost physically ill seeing him again, even though she had psyched herself up for weeks for this moment.

They alighted the wooden steps where once, 30 years previously, there had only been ragged stones as the foothold. As Meg climbed upward, she felt Jack's eyes on her from behind. The incline was steep and a least 15 metres high.

Breath rasped in her throat as they reached the top. Looking down on that familiar pattern of rocks was like looking into the past.

The taste of alcohol on Jack's tongue as he thrust it roughly into her mouth sobered Meg immediately. Meg tried to pull away, eyes darting to the pile of discarded cooler bottles.

She grabbed his forearms and pushed him off, heaving herself from the rock. "No, Jack."

"Come on, Meg, you know this is what you want."

"No," she protested frantically.

Anger flashed in Jack's eyes. "Get real. You've been after me all year. Ben is only second prize."

"He isn't." She spat the words at him. "He's better than you'll ever be."

The names Jack shouted at her as she scrambled up the cliff pelted against Meg like rocks. She had to try and explain this mess to Ben before Jack got there first.

"Do you remember that last party we had here, straight after the exams?"

Jack exhaled loudly and looked to the sky as if searching for the memory amongst the clouds.

"Hell, Meg, we had so many huge times here, it's hard to pick one from the other."

Meg forced a smile, hesitating for a second, before reaching one hand along his back. After all these years, Jack's muscles still felt taut under his shirt.

"Shall I remind you?" she asked.

. . .

Meg ran to school the next morning with hair still wet and head throbbing. Her stomach twisted in knots when she saw Ben's figure hunched at a lunch table, his lanky body looking suddenly out of place in the schoolyard.

For a moment she relaxed a little. Once she explained...the alcohol, the situation; surely things could get back to normal. And then she saw his face.

"I've seen Jack." His tone was flat, emotionless. "Is it true?"

"Ben, he's trying to break us up," she stammered.

"Is it true? Were you together at the Point last night?"

The calmness of his voice frightened Meg.

"Is it true?" Ben demanded again.

"Yes." Remorseful tears stung her eyes. "Ben, I'm so sorry."

The hysterical apology hung in the air as Ben slid out of the bench and disappeared like a ghost between two school buildings.

"Ben!"

Meg screamed his name as she raced after him.

Cate was standing at her locker. She looked up with a steely gaze as Meg approached.

"How could you do it Meg?"

"Where is he?"

"He ran through here before. Don't think he'll want to see you," Cate snapped. "Jack's already mouthed off to the whole school about you two getting it off at the beach last night."

Meg's head snapped up. "It was only a kiss Cate, a stupid kiss."

Cate looked stunned. "What? Jack's been telling him all about the great sex you had. No wonder Ben is freaking out."

Meg grabbed at Cate's arm. "Where is he?"

"The Point, Meg. Ben's gone to Echo Beach."

. . .

Jack was talking about his business prowess when he turned at the touch of Meg's hand on his back. Tears were streaming down her face, fingertips feeling dirty as they touched his skin. The smug smile that had appeared at her initial touch turned quickly to surprise as, in a smooth, quick movement that took every inch of her strength, Meg pushed Jack over the edge of the cliff.

Ben had taken his old Holden from the school car park and sped up the short road to the coast. Meg ran until exhausted and until the ambulance screamed past her, she had not given up hope of working the whole mess out.

By the time she arrived at Echo Beach, the paramedics were preparing to lower a stretcher down the rugged cliff. Strong arms of a fisherman, who had witnessed the whole tragedy and radioed for help from his car, held her back as she attempted to jump after Ben. In her hysteria she saw his crumpled body on the rocks below, that forelock of hair blowing in the ocean breeze.

Thirty years later, and it was Jack who lay mangled on the rocks, his mouth twisted in apparent surprise as a dark red stain leeched onto his highlighted hair. Calmly, Meg descended the stairs and retrieved her sandals from the boulder. She was careful not to step on the sand but couldn't help looking at Jack's lifeless body. Still, she felt nothing.

Meg jumped from the last rock into the water and walked quickly back up along the beach. Everything had gone pretty much to plan. No-one else had arrived for the reunion. Nor would they for another 24 hours. Every other invitation Meg had posted out anonymously listed tomorrow's date — except for Jack's.

Would his body be found before then? Who cared? It was vital she cleared her head when there was more urgent business to attend to. Waves drowned out her heartbeat as Meg paced briskly back toward her car, saltwater splashing up onto her legs. She didn't look back.

There would be police swarming all over Echo Beach tomorrow. Plain Meg Tudor would be just as shocked as the other old scholars of 1983 over the death of popular Jack Riggs.

The perfect crime? Meg doubted it. She'd watched enough crime investigation shows on TV to know there was bound to be a trace of her DNA somewhere. Hopefully, her attendance at tomorrow's reunion would explain that. And if she did get found out, so be it. She only needed another 24 hours. There was only one more thing that mattered.

Days passed like a blur. Meg was sick for months after Ben's suicide. While others were shocked at first, time moved on for them. Cate, Gail, Jack, they continued their lives, moved away, headed in new directions. Meg was offered a position at university but couldn't attend. As she slowly emerged from the fog of her grief, she was offered a job at the pharmacy. It was a sympathy offer, Meg knew that, but what choice did she have? She needed the money and the job was okay. Funny how days turned into weeks, then months, then years...

Meg was amazed at her calmness as she drove home, familiar turns in the road coming easily. She even managed a friendly wave to one of the customers from the pharmacy, although the hand that had pushed Jack to his death felt shaken and unclean.

Back at her house, she showered and put on the blue dress

and beads she had laid out on the bed earlier. She appraised herself in the mirror. *Not bad for a middle-aged woman,* she thought honestly. Ben flashed into her mind. How would he have looked at this age? How would have he felt on this day?

It was a short trip to her final destination where the spire of the Anglican Church reached into the cloudless heavens. Meg parked her car in the shade of an evergreen tree and walked briskly to the building entrance. At the steps of the church stood the man she loved more than any other in the world.

The relief on his face was obvious as she approached. Familiar green eyes looked nervous, but his face soon broke into a grin. She reached up to that unruly lock of hair and pushed it back from his forehead. He was the spitting image of his father.

"Mum, where have you been?"

Meg couldn't help but smile as her nervous son prepared to rush headfirst into marriage.

"Relax, Michael. You didn't think I'd miss seeing you stand up at the altar, did you?"

"Well, what have you been doing?"

"I just had a few things to tidy up."

"Couldn't it wait?"

Meg smiled. Some things had waited long enough.

A DEATH IN THE FAMILY

At first glance, it appeared to be a post-apocalyptic landscape.

Standing on blackened ground in the middle of a smoking paddock, Brevet Sergeant Amos Hughes scratched at his prematurely balding head. Around him, shafts of white smoke rose upward in thin spires, emanating from small stumps of wood and dried sheep shit.

"If I didn't know better Cliff, I'd find this whole thing pretty symbolic," he said.

Constable Cliff Rogers, recently seconded from the closest regional city, glanced quizzically at his superior. Symbolic? The situation was pretty weird, to be honest.

Merely a week ago, he had left the boredom of a front desk and now, only a metre away, was the scorched body of a local farmer, charred remnants of clothing melding with melted skin.

"They were burning off," Amos began vaguely.

In the short time he had been in the rural town of Harton, Cliff had become accustomed to Amos' smug habit of educating a city slicker such as himself in the ways of the land.

"Farmers do it every year, clearing the paddock of weeds and snails ready for next planting season."

"An accident then?" Cliff ventured. So far, he had chosen to not look too closely at the body.

Amos exhaled loudly and shook his head. "I don't think so Cliff, there's a gaping hole in his chest. Frank was shot, with a shotgun by the look of it. The fire didn't kill him. It raced over him quickly, no deep burns, most of his clothes are still intact."

Cliff thought of Frank's family, two grown sons and their wives, assembled back at the farmhouse with another police officer. Poor bastards.

The younger generation had gathered in this spot only a few hours previously, preparing to burn off the pasture paddock as a team. And now, the patriarch of iconic Hell's End Farm lay smouldering on the ground. How quickly life can change.

"Nice guy by all accounts?" Cliff asked.

"True blue local," Amos said. "The Berrin family has been in the district for years."

Cliff forced himself to glance down at the body. It lay on its side, one leg at an awkward angle, and its chin resting on his chest. What remained of Frank Berrin's wispy, grey hair had singed black against his head. Cliff looked away and wiped his mouth. Behind them another police car drove slowly into the paddock.

"Let's leave it to these guys," Amos said. "We need to get statements from the rest of the family."

Hell's End Farm had been held by the Berrin family for over a century. The main stone homestead was nestled amongst a towering stand of river red gums between the gentle rising slopes of two hills. Two smaller cottages, originally earmarked for workmen in the more profitable years of farming, were dwarfed by an assortment of sheds that had been randomly constructed over the years.

The long driveway that stretched to the main road was lined with pine trees planted by Jack Berrin to celebrate the birth of his only son in the years following the Second World War. A son was even more important than the end of this great conflict; Hell's End had a new generation.

Before this majestic line of trees grew large enough to shade the cars that motored in and out the gravel driveway, everyone in the district agreed that, whether the paddocks held sprightly lambs or were filled with rich golden wheat, Hell's End Farm was a beautiful place.

Which was why old Jack had come up with the name; it tickled his sense of humour. He enjoyed telling people he lived at Hell's End and then watched their surprise when they saw the beauty of the rich, brown land he farmed.

Sometime in the 1950s, he fashioned a name plate from a gum tree that had fallen in the corner paddock and spent a day in the workshop carving letters into the wood and staining it with black paint. The nameplate had hung on the dirt roadside ever since.

By the late twentieth century, Jack's son Frank had buried his father in the Harton cemetery and carried on the workload of Hell's End with his own two sons, Hamish and Greg. The boys were chips off the old Berrin block, the locals said, tall and lean as fence posts with the signature dark Berrin hair blended with a thoughtful set to their face like their mother.

The Berrin boys followed the endless agricultural cycle of spraying, seeding, shearing and harvesting, guided by the experience and wisdom of their father.

Then into the delicate equation came Paula and Alison, the

first women to set foot at Hells End since the death of the boy's mother, Ruth, some 15 years earlier.

Cliff had gotten this family tree run down on the ride out to Hell's End that morning.

"Bastard of a way for him go," Amos had commented before they left the smouldering paddock. "Can't imagine who would have it in for Frank."

Cliff may have been wet behind the ears, as Amos had informed him gleefully, but even he knew the first lesson of Murder 101 was to suspect those closest to the victim.

Greg and Hamish were large men at their full height, but as the police officers surveyed the group gathered in the lounge room of one of the farmhouses, the brothers sat together on the floral sofa like two lost boys.

To their right, a dark-haired woman sat cross legged, mouth set in a firm line. At 35, Paula Berrin retained features that attracted a second glance. Her troubled eyes watched her husband shift uncomfortably in his seat.

It was the same old lounge chair she had once settled into nervously for the first meeting with her future father-in-law, Paula thought suddenly. The lounge suite had long since been shunted out of the main farmhouse and passed to the next generation.

Unconsciously, Paula shuddered.

When she first met Hamish, Paula had been working in a bar. Hamish was visiting the city, attending a farm rally against some government regulation. He and some mates had worked up a thirst and wandered in to her workplace. Paula was living a university lifestyle that involved sex, alcohol and pizza.

"In that order," she flirted at the dark, brooding farmer

when he ordered drinks. She loved his arms from the outset, strong and tanned. Not to mention his slow, considered smile.

"What are you studying?" Hamish had asked.

"Media Studies," Paula said, flicking up the tap from the froth of the last beer.

"Any chance I can study you?" Hamish grinned.

From then on, Paula was a goner. She laughed at the location joke about Hell's Farm, and on her first visit could envisage the former glory of the homestead rose garden. She had looked forward to meeting the man whose son she was now in love with.

"Hamish, get Paula a coffee," Frank had said jovially as they sat awkwardly on the fabric-covered lounge that first day.

Frank was an older, shorter version of Hamish and his brother Greg. Paula had stared at the old man's gnarled hands resting on the arm of the chair. When Hamish disappeared into the kitchen, so did Frank's smile.

"I see you've got Hamish wrapped around your little finger,"

Apprehension stirred in Paula's stomach. "I wouldn't say that," she started uncertainly.

"Oh, I can see it alright. Just keep in mind you won't get your hands on an acre of this farm."

Paula still sat open mouthed when Hamish returned. Frank rose from the chair and plastered that Berrin smile back on.

"Lovely to meet you Paula," he said. "I'll leave you two to your coffee. Hope to see more of you here at Hell's End."

It was such a contrast, Paula was sure she must have mistaken Frank's sudden change. Soon though, she learnt better.

Despite this, media studies went out the window, and less than a year later, Hamish brought his bride home to one of the other houses on the property. Things were perfect. Except for Frank.

It was ironic that Greg met his future wife, Alison, on the corner of the same street where Paula had tended the bar, though the circumstances could not have been more different. Dark haired Greg, two years older but not as outgoing and cheeky as his younger sibling, had attended a friend's wedding at St Patrick's Church one Saturday afternoon in early winter.

As he watched the bride glide up the aisle, Greg fiddled with the unfamiliar tie that was wrapped around his neck, recalling his father's angry face as he had driven off from Hell's End that morning. Tractors were expected to be moving around the clock this time of year, drilling in the grain that grew the coming summer crop that provided their annual income.

In his pocket, a cigarette packet itched at his chest. He hated the way attempting to ignore his father's words only caused them to grow louder in his troubled mind. Eventually, he politely excused himself along the pew, escaped down the carpeted aisle and out into the cool breeze. Greg looked up at the clouds scudding across the sky. The weather was perfect for being on the tractor.

He was attempting to assuage his guilt by sliding a cigarette from the gold packet and had just struck a match when he saw her. At the front of St Patrick's, a young woman stood at the church sign, a piece of chalk in her slender fingers as she scribed something onto the blackboard. She was slender with blonde hair pulled up into a bun; tendrils had escaped and framed her heart shaped face. At that moment, she resembled an angel. The match burned back to Greg's fingers and he swore and tossed the match on the ground.

"No swearing by the Lord's house," the angel said with a small smile.

It was hard to tell if she was serious, but Greg had instantly forgotten his burnt finger, the farm — and everything else.

Her name was Alison; she was the daughter of the local Anglican minister, and in less than a year they were married in that same church, though tactfully avoiding seeding time.

Alison and Greg settled into the smaller house on the property.

A fortnight after marrying Greg, Frank ran into Alison outside the post office in town.

"I'll tell you now what I told Paula," Frank rattled, thrusting his mail key into the metal door of the post box. "You needn't think you're getting your hands on my farm,"

Alison's eyes opened wide. "Frank, I love Greg, it has nothing to do with Hell's End."

"Just so you're sure," Frank said. "The whole property will be going straight to my grandson."

"What grandson?" Alison asked.

Frank raised his brows to seal his meaning. Alison's lips parted slightly in shock — she and Greg had only been married two weeks!

But Frank had turned away, raising his hand to a woman across the street. "Good morning Eleanor," he called cheerfully. "Isn't it a lovely day?"

Paula had lived in the house to the east of the shearing shed for over a year before Alison moved to Hell's End. Paula wasn't sure what to make of the shy, religious woman at first and so they lived in an uneasy triangle; Frank in the main homestead, surrounded by the withering sticks of long neglected roses,

Paula and Hamish in the shadow of the corrugated iron shearing shed and Alison and Greg in the old stone workman's house tucked in amongst graceful, mottled gums. Although the atmosphere was ugly at times, Hell's Farm was indeed beautiful.

Paula found Alison friendly enough, though prone to quoting the bible. That could probably be expected from a minister's daughter, she told Hamish — after all, people stuck with what they knew. That's why former bar attendant, Paula, could mix a mean cocktail or select a good wine.

About two months after Greg and Alison moved in across the farmyard, Paula sat in the lengthening shadows on her veranda, enjoying the view of the dappled hill at sunset. Contemplating another evening alone, Paula saw Alison's kitchen light flick on. On each side of the houses two huge tractors droned their way around the paddock. Frank's ute was gone from his house, he was off checking the boys were running things as per his instructions.

Impulsively Paula grabbed a bottle of wine from the rack, a good red she had been saving for a special occasion. What better occasion than to get to know her new sister-in-law?

In less than a minute she was on Alison's veranda.

Alison opened the door hesitantly to see Paula invitingly shaking a bottle of wine, her eyes shining with anticipation. "I've got the wine if you've got the glasses."

Paula stared uncertainly. Her bible was open on the coffee table. It had been hard to break the habit of a nightly reading, but she doubted her new sister-in-law would understand that.

"Sure, thanks," she said hesitantly.

The old slab table at which they sat had come from one of the machinery sheds. Alison had sanded and polished it in the few weeks she had lived at Hell's End. Paula poured the wine into the glasses Alison had got from the cupboard, red liquid splashing up the side. The two women sat in uneasy silence on opposite sides of the table and sipped on their drinks. If Paula saw the bible, she didn't mention it. If Alison saw Paula's tattoo of a dragon peeking out from under the shoulder of her shirt, she didn't mention that either.

Though later they laughed that the alcohol loosened their tongues, the conversation meandered from the beauty of their new home to the pervasive, depressing influence of their father-in-law.

"I don't understand why Frank hates me so much," Alison said.

"Hates you?" Paula chuckled. "I've been here for over a year; you've got plenty more hate to look forward to." She smiled playfully at Alison. "I'm definitely not who he expected Hamish to marry," she continued, imitating Frank's deep voice and sarcastic manner. "Not that anyone would ever measure up."

Alison was emboldened by wine. "I'm not either, and Frank has no time for religion, he told me himself."

"But you didn't marry Frank," Paula teased.

"I know but, I mean," Alison stammered at first, nervous of this confident woman who was now part of her life. She caught the playful glint in Paula's eye just in time.

They laughed together, and Paula poured more wine.

By the early morning, when the smell of freshly dug earth wafted through the damp air from the tilled paddocks, Paula had made two trips through the trees to collect more wine. As she settled into bed and waited for Hamish to return from the paddock, Paula anticipated the arrival of a headache next day. But it was worth it to learn one of life's little truths.

Nothing makes a friend like a common enemy.

Alison and Paula quickly learned there was no such thing as a quiet time in a farmer's life. As sure as seeding followed spraying, windrowing the crops followed shearing. Paula and Alison helped each other survive the seasons. Once Pearl and Ivy arrived, Alison interspersed reading bible passages with making patchwork quilts for her new nieces.

Often at night, when she and Greg lay in their bed, conversation turned to the two little girls who bloomed in the house across the yard.

"I really want us to have a baby," Alison said softly.

"Me too. It will happen for us Alison, don't worry."

"But it's not," Alison said. "The doctor told me to avoid stress. And your Dad ... "

Greg sighed audibly in the darkened room. "Don't let Dad bother you. I know he can be harsh, but at heart he means well. It will all happen for us Alison. Have faith."

Greg rolled over. Alison lay with her eyes open for several minutes.

"Faith is the assurance of all things hoped for," she mouthed quietly.

The women didn't always suffer in silence. In mid-February, the day before the fire season opened, Paula decided to challenge Frank. After six years there were things that needed to be said.

"Things need to change around here, Frank. You need to change."

They faced each other at the homestead door; the stench of alcohol rose like a toxic cloud around Frank. Paula knew then it had been a mistake to come.

"You have no right to come up here and confront me," Frank spat, eyes narrowing.

"I own Hell's End," he went on smugly. "I'll do whatever I choose. You need to concentrate on what you're best at. Six years you're been here and only managed to produce two daughters, not even a son to carry on at Hell's End once I've gone. Though at least you've had some children — Alison is as barren as the Simpson Desert."

Paula's eyes blazed. "You have two sons, why can't they carry on with Hell's End?"

Frank laughed, his bloated face tossed back. Paula stared with repulsion at the spikes of grey stubble that sprouted under his chin. She turned and walked back across the farmyard to her daughters, wishing she had never wasted her time.

But, a day later, things were about to change.

In the morning, two utes met at the corner of the back paddock. Over the years, Paula and Alison had learned there were simple rules about burning off: fire was lit in a narrow band in the downwind corner of the paddock and the flames survived on drips of flammable liquid before taking off into the dry weeds. Then, pushed by the wind, flames crackled to the edge of the firebreak, where it died out before escaping its line of containment.

"Should burn pretty well," Hamish predicted, a slight breeze lifting his hair. "Where's the old man?"

Alison leant against the tray of the ute. It was unlike Frank to not appear to make sure things were being done correctly. "Thought he was meeting us out here at one?"

Greg tugged on his cap. "Haven't seen him all day."

Paula made no pretence of patience. "We can't wait around," she said. "I've got to go in town and do some shopping later."

Greg looked at his brother. "What do you think?"

"Make a decision for God's sake," Paula said. "Do you have to wait for Frank to decide everything?"

Paula got in the ute and slammed the door, aggravating her headache. The night before, with their husbands at a meeting in town, she and Alison had again shared a bottle of wine, discussing Paula's confrontation with their drunken father-in-law.

"She's right," Alison said tiredly. "Let's just get this paddock done."

Paula and Hamish took the first shift. Paula walked the length of the eastern side with the lighter, each drip of fuel creating tiny blazes in the paddock. Hamish followed in the ute, water pump thumping on the back, ready to put out any flames that crept across the break.

By the time Paula reached the corner, the smoke had become thicker. In the distance, through the grey shroud, she could see the lights of the other vehicle, and a new line of flame creeping up on the one she had just done. The concept of burning off had been novel to her initially, but now it was just another phase in the farming year.

In a few more sweeps, the paddock was totally ablaze, thick smoke fanned by the light winds. The trick now was to watch for whirly winds that threatened to take a burning ember into the next paddock. An embarrassing and stressful occurrence that brought the local CFS out in force and meant buying a round of drinks at the local pub the next Friday night.

The smoke was gone quickly, dying out as the flames ran out of fuel. Dotted around the smoking paddock, balls of smouldering sheep dung and small stumps of wood still let off plumes of smoke.

The two vehicles met up on the western side. Hamish and Paula had done a lap of the firebreak, checking for creeping lines of fire. The four of them got out, looking over the blackened paddock.

"That burned perfectly," Greg commented "Should we move to the next one?"

Hamish rubbed his chin with indecision, like his brother, he wasn't used to making a decision without Frank's derisive input.

Before he could speak, Greg pointed to the edge of stone heap a gentle rise in the southern edge of the paddock. An unusual amount of smoke rose from a shape on the ground.

"What's that?"

Paula screwed up her face as she tried to make out the shape. "Sheep carcass?"

"Better give it a squirt of water. We'll meet you in the next paddock in five."

Greg and Alison got in the ute and headed to the smoking pile. Hamish and Paula hadn't even reached the gate when Greg's shaking voice came across the UHF radio.

"Hamish, get over here."

The tone in his voice made Paula glance up at her husband.

Hamish shrugged and turned the ute to where his brother knelt on the faraway rise.

At first, as they drew closer, it looked like a pile of clothes was smouldering but then with a shock, they knew exactly what it was.

Hamish threw the ute door open. "What the hell ... "

And now, two hours later, Amos was whispering to his young associate in the kitchen of the Alison and Greg's cottage. "There's two shotguns registered on this property," he said softly. "The boys were at a meeting in town till about 11:30."

Cliff's eyes lit up. "Doesn't rule them out."

"No, but it gives us a timeline. Frank was alive at 10:30. He was on the phone," Amos paused. "To me."

Cliff raised his brows.

"Nothing suspicious," Amos said. "He was asking about fire regulations. If he suspected something, he didn't mention it." He shook his head. "Hard to believe one of these four is probably responsible."

"So, we have four suspects who will all alibi each other," Cliff summarised. "And if the killer waited for everyone else to be asleep, it could have been any one of them."

"Right," Amos said. "Let's get some statements."

Amos cleared his throat theatrically. "I can't begin to tell you how sorry I am about what's happened," he started. "Frank will be a great loss to the community and I can't imagine what effect his death will have on you."

Alison jumped up suddenly. "Coffee, can I get everyone coffee?"

Greg looked up at his wife, blank faced. "Sure, love."

"Alison, perhaps in a minute," Amos started, but the strange little woman had already gone through the door to the kitchen.

"She likes to keep busy," Greg said woodenly.

"No milk," Alison called from the kitchen. "Paula, can I just duck over to your place and grab some?"

Not waiting for a reply, Alison went out the door.

Milk was the furthest thing from Alison's mind. In fact, nothing had stayed long in her mind lately.

The doctor told her to calm down, not to stress and she would become pregnant in her own time. But there wasn't time. She had seen the way Greg looked at her lately, like an old dry ewe that was incapable of reproducing anymore. She had seen their sad eyes as they stood in the sheep yards, destined for market as their farm use had expired.

Alison grasped the handle of the old ute and climbed in, slammed the door and fired the engine to life. Greg she could deal with, but Frank was another story. On the insect-spotted windscreen she replayed the night before in her mind.

It wouldn't be long before the police discovered Frank's blood-spattered ute parked in the back machinery shed.

Alison had almost been asleep in her chair, soothed by the wine she had shared with Paula, when the rattling motor of a familiar ute sounded outside. She placed her bible on the side table and looked out the window. Frank sat in his ute, parked alongside the veranda. He had a beer in his hand and one arm crooked through the open window.

Alison froze, her skin crawling with the touch of her father-in-law's hands from his visit the week before, and the weeks before that. He had tried this on Paula as well, but she was made of stronger stuff, less compliant. And once he had forced himself on Alison the first time, he apparently saw no reason not to visit his daughter-in-law whenever Greg was out.

Lord, give me strength. Alison went outside into the hot, close evening air. The trees rattled in the slight breeze and cast dancing shadows across them.

"What do you want?" Alison demanded, trying to draw on the strength Paula always showed.

A leer pinched Frank's face and he fed it with a swig from the bottle. "I think you know," he slurred. He was drunker than usual. "That other useless bitch can only breed daughters, and you can't even breed anything."

Alison clenched the rear vision mirror with one hand. "Get out of here Frank,"

Frank threw his head back and laughed. "Since when do

you tell me what to do? Doesn't the bible say to go forth and multiply?"

Alison's grip stiffened, then past Frank's disgusting figure, her eyes settled on a shot gun resting on the passenger seat.

Frank followed her gaze. "Been shooting some rabbits out the north paddock with my new shotgun," Frank said. "Now I need to relax." He tried opening the door, but Alison pushed it shut defiantly.

"Bit of fight about you tonight hey? I don't mind that you know."

Alison was transfixed by the gun, bile rising in her throat.

"You wouldn't have the guts," Frank challenged.

And then, whether due to alcohol or stupidity, Frank passed her the weapon. Alison felt it in her hands, powerful and cold.

She had read about murderers saying that they didn't recall firing the weapon. And she now knew that to be true. While she expected the gun to be loaded, she didn't expect the noise to echo around the beautiful trees of Hell's End so much it sent a flock of sleeping galahs screaming into the air.

She wasn't prepared for the size of the gaping hole that opened up in his chest either or the small groan that escaped Frank's bitter mouth. Still holding the weapon, Alison's head snapped over to Paula's house, which remained shrouded in darkness. After her argument with Frank, Paula had probably polished off another bottle of wine and put herself to bed. Alison was glad, Paula had been a lifesaver, and she didn't want her implicated in this.

Calm came over Alison then, a feeling she hadn't experienced since her former life around St Patrick's.

She pushed Frank's bulk across the seat, an arc of blood smearing across the vinyl. Climbing into the driver's seat, she drove the ute back to the machinery shed, dry retching as she travelled the short distance behind Frank's house. When Greg and Hamish returned a short time later, she made Greg a cuppa and popped in a few of those pills the doctor told her would help her sleep.

At 2:00 am, she stole silently through the farmyard and back into Frank's ute. His body lay across the seat, as grotesque in death as he had been in life. She knew the back paddock was slated for the first burn the next morning. She drove on adrenalin and pushed the body out at the edge of a stone heap. His head clunked against a rock and collapsed like a sack of potatoes. Alison felt nothing.

And now the police were here. Couldn't they see that because of Frank's death, a morbid coat of darkness had been shrugged off the shoulders of Hell's End?

Still, Alison's heart felt heavy as she turned the steering wheel. She had no intention of getting milk and she didn't plan to answer any questions when she knew she couldn't lie.

Alison turned into the beautiful pine lined driveway of Hell's End. At the end of the driveway she paused, considering options.

Was there a time she could pinpoint the start of this nightmare? The first time Frank had visited her? Greg's inability to stand up to his father? One shaking hand settled on her stomach. Or was it the fact that the only child she could carry was that of her father-in-law?

Alison only knew for certain that she and Paula were prime suspects. Paula had been her only solace in this place and Alison wouldn't have suspicion cast upon her.

Words floated through Alison's head. *Thou shalt not kill.*

Though she initially planned to, Alison suddenly realised she could never return to her former life at the church.

For a moment, she idled undecided at the gateway, the ute thrumming with apparent impatience. In the distance along the dirt road, a semi-trailer, loaded with sheep destined for the market, crested the hill. It gave Alison time to think. In the seconds as it came closer, she made her decision.

It would be obvious soon, Alison thought, as she planted her foot on the accelerator and sped out onto the road past the carved Hell's End sign.

The collision could be heard back at the farmhouse. As Cliff took a statement from Hamish Berrin, a sickening, final twisting of metal echoed along the picturesque driveway.

They will know it had to be me was Alison's final thought as the truck impacted the side of her vehicle.

Surely it was obvious as soon as they saw the blistering skin and shrivelled hair on Frank's body.

After all, shouldn't the Devil burn in Hell?

THE IRONY OF SILENCE

WINNER: BODY IN THE LIBRARY, SCARLETT STILETTO AWARDS, 2020

Laura

A library is more than a home for books. For some it is a refuge.

This thought, not so random, passed through Laura's mind as she swept the returned books from their dumping space and into her arms. Spreading them out on the wooden desk, she reached out for the black, plastic scanner with its infrared eye. Charged with opening the Mulga Gardens Library doors first thing in the morning and locking them at night, the first and last hour of each day was a welcome, quiet repose.

It was bookend hours in a way; these first and last hours marked each side of six work hours when Bruce Pecker was librarian-in-charge. In those six hours, Bruce felt it his duty to educate his younger workmate with such condescending politeness that Laura was tempted to swipe the dark-rimmed glasses from his face. But she wasn't into violence. Quite the opposite.

These precious hours were a buffer from the dramas of

home where Mike compressed and interrupted her life in a different and harsher way than Bruce ever could.

A hardcover slipped from her grip, clipping her forearm before landing open on the carpet, pages splayed. In this blissful, early hour, there was no need to check if anyone spotted her slight, painful wince. Laura pulled down her sensible blouse sleeve to hide the bruise.

Too much pepper in the casserole last night. Her fault entirely.

The daily escape to this building of a thousand stories never lost its appeal. It was quiet — not silent as demanded in libraries of the past, but peaceful all the same. Laura amused herself with an internal guessing game, predicting the favoured genre of new customers. She rolled this silly game around her mind like a kid with a boiled lolly that never lost its flavour. The regulars were predictable by now; Nola Clancy, a university professor who enjoyed the neat and happy endings of cheap romance novels, ex-army rifleman, John Campbell, who soaked up every biography and family history stalwart, Clancy Stern, who was hot on the non-fiction section. But there was one regular she could never put a finger on. Indi Samson.

Laura only knew this woman's name by checking her library card. How long ago now? Six or eight weeks? Indi Samson was there after Laura had gotten out of hospital with that broken rib. Slipped on the mossy path, she explained to Bruce. Her fault entirely.

Anyway, in that sacred first hour, holding her side as she came out of the tiny work kitchen with a steaming green tea, Laura had laid eyes on her. Around 40, she was dressed in a careless boho style that looked thrown together and fashionable all at the same time. To be honest, Laura was initially drawn by her style. Laura was required to look like a staid librarian — not that work demanded that, but Mike did. In contrast, if she had to sum up Indi Samson's style in one word, it would be quite simple. Free.

From that day on, Indi was the first customer of every morning, already browsing the shelves when Laura exited the kitchen with her morning cup of tea. Annoyed at first by this intrusion to her hour of peace, Laura soon realised she wasn't about to be bothered with unrequested book reviews or pleas of recommendation of a certain genre.

Firstly, because this boho woman didn't have a certain genre, she had many. From science fiction to romance, horror to non-fiction — she borrowed them all.

Secondly, in three months, Indi Samson had never uttered a single word.

Indi

Mulga Gardens wasn't the first library Indi had spent so much time in. When her fingers skimmed the books, she felt familiar safety in the countless endings of everyday stories. Books offered possibilities.

Originally, Indi had doubted if this particular building was a suitable place for her. In the first few days, a middle-aged man with balding hair and hooded eyes had stood behind the desk. She quickly recognised his suspicion, glancing up occasionally as though she was about to thrust a leather-bound first edition into her handbag. Not that this library had first editions or that she had a handbag — well not really, rather a loose string thing where she carefully stacked her daily borrowings.

And then Laura had appeared, ordained with a glossy, plastic name-tag, which was decorated with children's stickers and affixed to her blouse with horizontal perfection. Indi was immediately aware of the carefully trained, vacant gaze and her too tight grip on the steaming beverage — every day in the same cup, at the same time. Such predictability worked in Indi's favour.

Once, with her back to the borrowing desk, one hand sliding along the line of books, Indi studied the librarian's reflection in the glass door. Laura bent slightly to the left and massaged her ribs more than once, followed by a slow exhalation of breath. When Indi borrowed books, the librarian's fingers lingered on the covers as if bidding them farewell. But the books were always back safely the next day. Once, early on, Laura had tried to strike up conversation. "Gosh you read a lot of books," she had said brightly. Indi had met her eyes briefly, but not replied. The next day Laura held up a book and said, "I've heard this was a good one."

With no reply but noting a slight smile forthcoming, Laura had extended herself to open-ended questions. Indi remembered them from school, ones which required more than a yes or no answer. Internally, she gave Laura points for trying but offered nothing as a reward.

She wasn't trying to be rude. Indi wasn't trying to be anything but invisible. But as a regular morning and afternoon visitor to the library she knew she had become recognisable. Ideally though, becoming a regular also makes you invisible, part of the furniture. Like the knitting club on Wednesday afternoons or the family history group who coveted all the computers on Tuesday mornings.

Indi had always found a comforting regularity in libraries — books coming in, placed on the shelves, resting and then going out again. At Mulga Gardens Library, she discovered they had regular library displays (overseen by arbitrary Bruce, she noticed) changing dependent on the time of year or based around a recently released novel or visiting author. Indi sensed

Laura found comfort in this reliable monotony. She recognised that sameness about her. But over time, though still overtly interested in Indi's choice of books, Laura had eventually given up trying to make conversation.

As weeks passed, even the piercing eyes of Bruce ignored Indi. Probably just as well he was not there to notice her predictable movements at the end of the day. As a bonus, Laura was always preoccupied, her brow furrowing and eyes clouding over as the clock marched toward five. Once, early on, Laura noticed at the last minute that Indi was still walking amongst the shelves. She hustled Indi out, the librarian's mind already in a far more precarious place as she pressed the alarm code and locked the door.

And never did Laura notice that at precisely 4:55 pm. every day, just before closing, Indi was always by the audio book shelf, nestled beneath the northern window.

Laura

Bruce has noticed her.

In those blissful silent hours, the peace before and after chaos, Laura's boss had made an unwanted and unnecessary appearance.

"Who's that?" he demanded. A compete catalogue of regular visitors was imprinted on his brain.

And yet, he didn't notice the obvious — the wince of pain as Laura leant over, the fading green bruises that were quickly replaced with new ones. Laura shrugged; for some reason, she chose to protect this mysterious visitor, though from what she wasn't sure.

Laura never mentioned Indi's complete silence. The mysterious boho woman never approached the desk when Bruce was there and Laura knew why. She recognised familiar flickering eyes, hastily avoiding contact, dancing a frantic tango.

But the books! Indi borrowed at least five a day and always returned them promptly the next morning. Like Laura, her mysterious customer always lingered longer at days end, fingering through the audio books, even though there was never one in her borrowing pile. Obviously not deaf then, but maybe mute? No word was uttered from her lips. Ever.

It didn't matter really; Laura was content with her mysterious customer's cautious smile and didn't bother with offering superfluous questions anymore. She remained close mouthed, just as Indi did, liking the fact that it was no business of others what dangers flirted at the edge of people's lives. Laura couldn't help but watch her though, this kindred spirit. Indi drifted along the shelves of fiction, non-fiction, magazines, YA, even the ancient microfiche containers. Not many libraries had microfiche anymore and fewer people even knew what they were — ancient, comparatively labour-intensive machines that required seeking out a flimsy black negative that held a thousand files and had to be inserted into a double glass plate, requiring a thousand more finger flicks than the internet.

After a few weeks, Laura found herself seeking out the flowing skirt and purple hemp scarf of her visitor. She was always the same; her brown hair falling across one eye, acting as a handy screen to society. Laura also knew what it was to want to hide from the world. She tried to unravel Indi's mystery by checking her borrowings but no go; sometimes it was classics, other times self-help, occasionally the odd biography or satisfying crime of retribution but nothing that spelled out and defined this mysterious person, and although she always finished her visit by the audio books, there was never a plastic covered CD in the pile. And so, every afternoon, just before closing, Laura scanned Indi's books, always trying to locate a pattern in her reading while also attempting to ignore the biting pain that chewed at her ribs.

INDI

Indi sensed why Laura hadn't tried too hard to figure her out. The librarian was enjoying her mysterious appearance as a distraction from reality, and Indi understood entirely. But while Indi didn't speak, she constantly listened. Bruce, the little arse, spoke with flippant, dismissive throwaway lines and Laura, to her credit, ignored all of them.

And when face to face, with expressions carefully vacant, Laura never spoke to Indi directly, rather to the desk, chair, telephone or carpet. Laura's comments to these inanimate objects cryptically told Indi that life at work was far better than at home, and she wasn't about to sabotage that by breaking the silence. Even yesterday, when Laura had announced the upcoming pearling industry display, featuring a unique smoky pearl from Western Australia as the centrepiece, Indi said nothing.

As for the daily load of books, Indi jammed them in her string bag every night and then emptied onto the desk every morning where Laura's immaculate nails swept them to the scanner. Indi skimmed most of them overnight — some were good, some average. There was a world of stories in every corner of the library; mags, novels, DVDs, even microfiche. You never knew what you might find out.

Indi's favourite time was at night; the darkness cloaked the day's exposure in a calming dark sanctuary. Not that these days her nights were totally dark. Dull maybe, but the security lights glowed through Indi's fitful sleep. And then there were the cushions ... an assortment of kid's characters and more mature greens and blues. This comfort of routine had slowed her racing thoughts.

The librarian, Laura ... Indi noticed how her brow wrinkled whenever she took in the boho outfit, as though it symbolised freedom, and this breezy clothing did, in a way. In actual fact, Indi had purchased her clothes at the local Salvos and was quite surprised that they had come across as retro fashionable — go figure. And all along, Indi already had Laura's number and could interpret her thoughts. This transparency wasn't Laura's fault of course, she just wasn't familiar with a life of dodge and adaptation. Or so Indi assumed at first.

In Indi's experience, it was worse when abuse came as a surprise not an expectation. But, as usual, she said nothing. And while it might seem unusual to be in the library every night and every morning, it was hardly against the law. As long as the books were returned before their due date then all was well, in spite of small-man-syndrome Bruce's odd looks over his glasses.

And by the end of the day, Indi felt as exhausted as Laura looked — except Laura was heading home to some abusive arsehole husband and Indi was preparing to settle down on a collection of random cushions that soothed her soul. She longed to tell Laura there were alternatives.

Laura

That woman, the casually fashionable one, Indi, was like clockwork. As usual, the last opening hour of the library attracted few customers, but Indi moved around the aisles, her long skirt making a whooshing sound. Laura wanted to tell her so many things, maybe because Indi didn't speak and there would be no pointed questions to answer.

The regularity of Indi's presence — a calm contrast to Laura's reality — had become a comfort, something soothing in her messy life. And then, one Thursday, while straightening the plastic cases of the audio books, Laura looked out into the courtyard and suddenly realised part of Indi's mystery. But, more than that, she appreciated and understood it.

That night, when Indi plonked her usual swag of books on the counter, Laura really looked at the titles for the first time. Seeking a clue, searching for some further interpretation of this mysterious person. But this time, whether Indi listened or not, there were things to say.

"We've got new pillows and cushions in the kid's area," Laura's words were flippant, but Indi read their intent. When you never spoke, every murmur, every noise had a nuance. You noticed things, like the sudden tension in Laura's hand as she turned the book over and the slight intake of breath. It was a new book, with a unique audience.

A title by former Prince Harry and Megan Markle — *Finding Freedom*. Indi's pale eyes didn't avert as usual but held Laura's in a knowing gaze. Coincidence that at that exact moment Laura's previously shattered rib ached like hell?

Their eyes found each other briefly and then snapped apart. It was Laura's turn to send a subtle message. As usual the conversation was with herself, with the desk, to the scanner waving through the air.

"Can you believe, we have an important security update? The old alarm code was Bruce's birthday, Australia Day 1972 ... 260172." The pile of leaflets on the counter were addressed next. "Not anymore though, it's his wedding anniversary now.

Who would imagine someone would go there? Anyway, 23rd of April, 2019 — 230419."

Laura chatted on as though no one was listening. Just when she thought she had worked this strange woman out, she realised that Indi sensed her secrets too. Didn't want to over-think it though. Had enough to worry about.

And then, over *Finding Freedom,* their eyes met once more. Understanding through silence. Until Laura said these words. Because, of course, Indi didn't speak. "That exhibition about the pearling industry — it opens next week. Bruce has organ-ised some expensive display pieces and so we will have a secu-rity guard in overnight. Thought you might want to know."

Indi

Sometimes Indi wondered if her choice of the strawberry shaped felt pillow with its sewn-on seeds was immature. But, as she nestled her head into the softness, next to the cushion puppy and the dinosaur, who really cared? There was a secu-rity with this warmth, dull lights and lines of books like body-guards at attention. Indi loved the library, day *and* night.

Laura's apparently flippant announcement that a security guard was going to invade her space was not welcome. Mulga Gardens Library was more than a sanctuary for mornings or afternoons, over time, this library had become a home. Early on it was a challenge, loitering by the audio books while tetchy fingers worked nimbly with the window latch. And then, with the last stragglers, she had left the library.

At first, Laura was on guard about this, but Indi's deliber-ately homely appearance had muted the fact that she may be a threat. Indi had become good at reading expressions, a genius almost, her past life had seen to that. She could pinpoint the exact moment that realisation crossed Laura's face. Even while choosing her evening reading, Indi never relaxed her guard around fellow customers. They were seemingly mostly pleasant, unsuspicious individuals, but who really knows?

And then, once she had unlocked that window, she walked out the main door just before Laura locked it. Then, Indi doubled around the back, slithered herself through the glass opening and sprinted to log in the alarm code. But tonight, Indi's evening was not as relaxed as normal. Even the strawberry pillow wasn't cutting it. The thought of a security guard conjured images that were actually quite the opposite. Even Laura, with hidden issues that Indi read like one of the thousand books on the library shelves, had lifted her eyebrows in warning. Indi was not happy with this security guard's upcoming intrusion. Freedom had become of her own making. She considered heading back out on the streets, but not for long; there was now someone more broken than she was. Books had become Indi's way of communication. *Finding Freedom* — it was a message for herself, as well as Laura.

LAURA

Indi's fingernails were dirty as she slid the book across the counter. They rested in contrast to Laura's immaculate manicure, hovering just under the title. Her grip submitted a subtle pressure that Laura released the book from, unaware that Indi had spent sleepless hours finding the right self-help title from an author she had never heard of. '*Make the Change*'. Laura's eyes snapped up, but Indi's were already trained to meet them with a grey-green gaze that held everything and nothing all at the same time.

And the next book 'A Room of One's Own' by Virginia Woolf. There was no doubt now, but though Indi had seen through the hideaway sleeves and a need to apply blue-grey eyeshadow on days like this, Laura needed Indi to know she wasn't the only one to discover secrets. Before locking up last night, Laura had rearranged the cushions in the kid's corner, burying the bright, felt strawberry way beneath. As she looked past the thin shoulders of her first and last visitor of the day, she could see it was on top. Now, there was no question as to how Indi made it through the door every morning without Laura noticing.

"We have a guard in here from tonight. Bruce is setting up the pearl display today. Quite a fancy specimen apparently," Laura said brightly, addressing the computer screen as the scanned books flashed across it. "The security guard will be here all night of course."

"Bruce can be so annoying," Laura said conspiratorially to the scanning device. "But I have to hand it to him, these regular displays do bring a lot of interest. Not often we need a guard to come with it though."

Silence, but what else did she expect. Guard, guard, guard — was Indi getting the message? Her hiding spot wasn't safe tonight.

"I'm leaving the kitchen unlocked .... for him." Laura slid the books across the counter. "There's some food in the fridge that needs to be eaten."

The words hung in the air. It was Indi's turn to break the gaze. Shuffling the books into the net bag, she bowed her head and went to the door. "Have a nice day," Laura said to the counter top. "See you this afternoon."

Indi

The park was crowded that day; families were taking advantage of the late spring sun and the flowers that popped with colour in the well-maintained gardens. For a long time, Indi had forgotten about colour, during a time when life was a muted grey, internally at least. Books had taken her away from all that, both then and now; amazing how a riot of colour can spring from black words on a white page. She had always frequented libraries, haunted them maybe, drifting along the aisles like a silent ghost.

Mulga Gardens Library was different. Besides Laura, the librarian, and Bruce, the very caricature of a male librarian, bespectacled, officious, talking to himself among the shelves, there were other quaint touches to the place. One wall cele-brated history; the opening by the then Governor of South Australia, the storm in the '50s that broke through the roof and flooded the non-fiction section and memories recorded by the archaic old microfiche, a relic of the past that also, ironically, linked people to the past.

Though Laura had hidden her latest bruise with eyeshadow, Indi spotted the broken capillaries that stained the whites of her eyes. Again, Indi had fought this connection to a kindred spirit. Bonding with people was dangerous. Normally, the unwanted intrusion of an overnight guard would have seen Indi choose another place to spend the night.

She had spent plenty of nights curled in doorways or beneath bushes in this very park, sleeping like a wild animal, never fully relaxed, a watchful eye on the world at all times.

She had become too smart for that though, and empty houses and sheds had been a step up for a while. Until the library, which now seemingly provided food as well as shelter. Indi's stomach rumbled at the thought. She withdrew the books from the dirty string bag, but tossed them aside on the wooden seat. After all, she hadn't really chosen them for herself.

Laura

There is an irony in silence. Not speaking can yell volumes.

While Laura prattled on all day at work, she prayed the evenings would rush by, hardly opening her mouth. It was dangerous to tempt the Devil. Stacking the dishwasher in their second floor flat, Laura found herself wondering if the same thing lay behind Indi's silence. Fear. It had a way of shutting you down, turning you into an internal being.

Sliding the plates in, careful not to clink them together, Laura took a deep breath. He, Mike, hadn't even noticed last night's leftovers were nowhere to be seen. Butter chicken. She hoped Indi liked it. After work drinks had clouded Mike's observation skills.

In this tiny flat, there was no escaping him, but as Laura pressed the button to launch the dishwasher into life, she heard beer induced, grumbling snores. Sometimes alcohol could be a blessing.

Tonight, at least, she was safe. And her thoughts flew to the library.

Indi

Her late afternoon visit was usually uneventful, but today, bustling Bruce had the eastern corner transformed with fishing nets and sea creatures. If she spoke, Indi would be tempted to tell him pearls weren't found in nets. But she had long stopped caring about other people's issues. At least until recently. And then, just before 4 o'clock, the highlight of the display arrived — a perfect grey-green ball formed by the wonder of nature and nestled on a velvet cushion in a locked glass cabinet. Laura had left her desk and peered at it for several long minutes. Indi stood there too and, as usual, conversation was one sided and directed at an inanimate object.

"Such a beautiful thing," Laura said dreamily." A little shrug was accompanied by a short outtake of breath. "I have a pearl in my engagement ring," she said.

But Indi, adept at noticing things, had never seen that on her slender fingers. Laura said nothing further. She had learnt, Indi realised, that not all feelings need vocalising to give them life.

There was no pretence of checking out books tonight. Laura caught Indi's eye in the fantasy aisle and offered a slight smile before dimming the lights and closing the door. No alarm required with a security guard due soon to watch over the illuminated cube and its treasure. The children's cushions had been moved to a side room — lockable, Laura had told the desk earlier while Indi lingered nearby. And the kitchen door, she reminded the chair, had been left open.

Butter chicken. One of Indi's favourites. She ate ravenously in the darkened study room, senses heightened when she heard the door click open. A large man, clad in a brown security outfit, strode into the lit corner. Indi peeked through the vertical blind. He bent to peer in the illuminated cube, yawning slightly. A sliver of light caught on an angular jaw and bulbous nose. He turned and Indi shrunk back, chicken now sour in her mouth. The strawberry cushion had gone rotten. There was something else she needed in the kitchen. Urgently.

Laura

Loneliness takes many forms, Laura thought as she slammed her car door, the library building looming in the distance. Indi was probably less lonely than she was, in a relationship that rotated on fear and subservience. Would the security guard have scared Indi away? Laura hoped not.

And then, unexpectedly, there she was. The mysterious boho woman. For the first time, Laura was seeing Indi outside of the library. She appeared even smaller and frailer in the light of day. The parcel Indi silently handed over was shrouded in a plastic shopping bag. Laura could feel the rigid spines of hardcover books and instinctively knew the question in her eyes would never have an answer. Because, right then, Indi turned and stepped quickly away. It was goodbye, Laura knew it. The guard had ruined everything.

Fiddling with her key, Laura let herself in the silent building and flicked on the bank of lights. Later, she would be glad she hadn't looked around first. She emptied the books on to the desk, breath catching in her throat as she read the titles. Agatha Christie's 'The Body in the Library' and 'The Pearl Thief' by Fiona McIntosh.

INDI

Walking quickly through the park, Indi turned the grey-green bauble over and over in her pocket until she imagined her fingerprints had worn off. Which would be handy considering her history, Indi thought, allowing herself a rare moment of humour. Libraries had always been a refuge, ironically requesting silence, when over the years she had become the very epitome of it. But Mulga Gardens Library had, quite surprisingly, been a cure as well. And not just for herself. Silence was ironically full of information.

LAURA

There was no doubt now that being a bad judge of character was a flaw in her personality. First in life partners and then in a total stranger. Laura had foolishly imagined a kindred spirit in the boho woman and had even allowed her refuge, and for what? Turns out she was nothing but a common thief and Laura's fanciful notion of this mute delivering messages through book titles had been ridiculous — until that last morning anyway.

Bruce had gone ballistic. Removal of the body of the security guard bought the type of publicity he precisely didn't want. As the local press reported, the guard had been stabbed by a knife from the library's kitchen and the pearl stolen. CCTV had saved Laura from suspicion, clearly showing an intruder in a flowing purple dress creeping up behind the hapless guard and stabbing him in the neck. But Laura decided to take a leaf out of Indi's book and stay silent. With a practiced blank face, she told the police investigator she had no idea who this woman was. Perhaps she still admired Indi in some way. Maybe that was why Laura crammed an overnight bag with her most precious possessions when leaving for work that morning.

Unexpectedly, a parcel awaited her. It was left outside the library by an overnight courier and scrawled with an unsteady hand — *Laura Librarian*. Inside, she found a book often requested by those looking for answers. Page 24 of '*The Secret*' spouted advice to project your greatest desires into the universe. It was marked with a flimsy microfiche slide that Laura recognised form the box in the corner. On it, a sticky note, clearly from her own library desk, penned with 'E14'. Crossing the room as the lights flickered to life, Laura slipped the negative into the slide, guiding the clunky apparatus to E14 where a page of the Adelaide Advertiser was illuminated, dated twenty years previously.

Guard arrested in prison rape — dismissed from job.

With the expert eyes of a skim reader, Laura absorbed the main points. The black and white photo showed the blurry image of a girl with frail features and a man, whose angular face and bulbous nose Laura had seen most recently covered in blood on the library floor. Laura returned to her desk, located some scissors and cut the microfiche into a thousand jagged pieces.

It was then that Laura noticed another envelope, its grubby corner poking from page 101 where *The Secret* encouraged the reader to live their best life. The bank cheque was made out in her name and for an amount that made Laura sharply draw breath. Who knew the pearl was worth so much?

Then, she clutched her overnight bag and headed back to the entrance. There was no point waiting for Bruce and offering any type of excuse for her sudden absence.

Silence had a way of conveying volumes.

SEE THE LIGHT

STATEMENT OF RUTH CRISP (DECEASED)

Would you be shocked to know that I wasn't surprised to be murdered?

After all, no one has ever really liked me. What really amazes me is that the two people I most expected to push me from the balcony outside the lantern room of the Thorpe Island Lighthouse were instead staring up at me as I fell, genuine horror contorting their faces.

It's a great view from up top, almost all the island is visible; trees, sand and rock mostly, with the addition of three 150-year-old and suitably rickety lighthouse keeper's cottages built in the centre clearing.

Thorpe Island seemed huge to me as a child, as things do. That's over sixty years ago now, when my Uncle Stan manned the lighthouse. He was in charge of maintaining the ray of safety that arced endlessly through the night around what, in the clear eyes of adulthood, is really just a tiny rocky outcrop in the Southern Ocean.

I spent most of my summer holidays here as a girl, playing with my cousin Sophie. I wasn't impressed with my enforced vacations at first, but Sophie wouldn't give up trying to impress me. "See the Light, see the light," she squealed excitedly on the first morning of every visit. Begrudgingly, I took in the towering stone pillar that was the focal point of the island. It never impressed me as much as Sophie hoped.

Still, we played hide and seek endlessly, the seeker required to count to sixty up on the lighthouse balcony. Crouching down on a narrow rim of metal, hiding from the wind and covering our eyes, added a dimension of danger to our childhood games.

Time moved on of course, and I haven't seen Sophie for a long time. Thorpe Island is now owned by the National Parks Service. For years I have considered hiring out the cottages for a family vacation with my sons. Then, just last month, my friend Henry noticed an article in the newspaper.

We were in the kitchen at the local bowling club, while outside white figures moved slowly up and down the green. As I assembled scones on plates, Henry quoted me bits of the Saturday paper. To be honest, I didn't pay a lot of attention until a familiar name caused my ears to prick up.

"It says here Thorpe Island won't be available for hire after the end of September."

"What's that, Henry?"

"Thorpe Island," he said, "isn't that the place you're always talking about?"

For a moment I was annoyed that, considering all the Saturdays we spent together, Henry hadn't taken better notice of my childhood stories.

"Of course, I haven't been there since I was twelve, you know that."

"Well, you won't have a chance unless you book soon, it's all closing down. Maintenance costs or something."

I'd never heard anything so ridiculous. While it hadn't been surprising that Uncle Stan eventually left Thorpe Island or that the light became automatic in the early 1980s, the possibility of me returning had always seemed likely. Until now.

I clicked on the mixer on the kitchen bench, whipping cream to stiff perfection for the scones.

"I'll book in on Monday," I yelled over the noise. "It's my birthday next month; I'll make it an event for my 70th."

I invited my sons of course; Roger and Pete. My sons are in their forties and poor Roger's had a few hassles of late, so I thought he would especially enjoy the break. Thorpe Island is the perfect place to relax and forget your troubles.

Of course, this meant they expected to bring their wives, Julie and Fran. Those girls have never liked me or the huge part I play in my son's lives. To be truthful, not many people seem to like me. They can't handle someone who would rather tell the truth to their face instead of offer up obsequious smiles and small talk.

It's true, I like to be right. This is why the bowling club's first division ladies' team had chosen to disclude me from their team last year. They didn't believe that my bowl, a semi-final decider, had been skewed by the wind. I was simply correcting the angle to make things fair when I touched it ever so gently.

The only people I truly trust are my sons, but I belatedly learned I shouldn't have told them about my visit to the lawyer, Mr Posonby, last week. I simply wanted to ensure my money goes to my boys only, once their wives leave them (and they will!).

Seems it's not an easy thing to ensure, what with people challenging wills and everything. It was going to take another week to make things watertight but, with the break on Thorpe

Island bang in the middle of all this, at least I had the chance to relax. Or so I thought.

Can you believe the boys told Julie and Fran? Apparently, their wives were furious and threatened not to travel to Thorpe Island for my birthday trip. Stupid girls. Can't they understand that, if they stay with their husbands, the money will be theirs as well, thanks to modern day laws that Mr Posonby tried to explain to me.

Is understanding too much to ask these days?

As we bumped our way from the mainland to Thorpe Island, those ungrateful girls didn't even utter a word. I knew as soon as I stepped onto the familiar sand that a climb to the top of the lighthouse would calm me down, as it always did as a child. I counted the 93 sandstone steps on my struggle upward. It was certainly a lot easier when I was a girl but worth it when I stepped onto the metal platform and inhaled a big breath of salty air. There were so many memories here.

But a person like me never truly relaxes. I watched from above as Fran clunked her suitcase up the steps of the cottage they were staying in, carelessly chipping paint from the veranda post. A moment later, Julie came out of the hut she was sharing with Roger with a glass of scotch and ice in her hand. Typical.

When I mentioned her constant drinking again last week, Julie was furious. If looks could kill! Fran was no better when I tried to explain Julie's bad behaviour. She muttered something about minding my own business. I told her she could go back to all that psychic crap she cares so much about. Tarot cards, crystals! What a load of garbage. I don't deserve such an ungrateful family. I admit I like things my own way. I always have, but what's wrong with that?

The crisp sea air did its job, clearing my mind as I hoped. Peering over the railing, I remembered the row of spindly yellow daisy bushes that Sophie and I had planted years ago. Leaning forward, I tried to pinpoint that particular base of our childhood energy.

I wasn't surprised to feel a soft presence in between my shoulder blades. At first it was as gentle as the ocean breeze but gradually increased in pressure until I found myself overbalancing against the rail.

On my swift, fatal fall to the earth below, I had time to see the astonished faces of both Fran and Julie. My only thought before I hit the ground was, I can't believe it wasn't them!

Statement of Julie Crisp

Angry waves tossed themselves against the jutting rocks that fringed Thorpe Island in much the same way I splashed the scotch into my glass; messily but with purpose.

"The only difference is the waves smash the rocks and you just plan to get smashed," Roger had commented caustically as he dropped our bags on to the double bed.

"Do you blame me?" I asked.

With precise and practiced action, I swirled the ice and amber liquid before taking a huge gulp. The warm sensation on my throat was instantly calming. Thank God for the filled ice trays I discovered in the freezer of the tiny fridge that whirred away efficiently in the corner.

Roger unzipped our bag and fussed over the contents, sliding out folded shirts as though he may need to don a tie at any moment. Being a doctor, he can never fully relax, but by now I'm used to it. A rim of silver edged his once black hair but he stood as upright and imposing as he had when we met in a bar in Greece twenty years earlier.

To be honest, I felt I owed it to him to make the journey out to Thorpe Island, his aggravating mother's childhood playground. Hoping vainly for a resort, the small rocky outcrop was ultimately disappointing, but a scotch improves any situation, the clinking ice immediately soothing my jangled nerves. Everyone has to have a vice, I figure.

The journey out had been rough, the boat skipper's skin wet with the salty waves as he wished us a good weekend before returning to the mainland. Our bags, two small ones due to the size of the boat we motored out on, had barely hit the worn carpeted floor of the lighthouse keeper's cottage before I retrieved the scotch bottle from its cushioned surround.

When did Johnnie Walker become my best friend? Ironically, it was well before the malpractice suit against Roger that had surfaced six months ago. Roger hadn't seemed overly affected at first, but now, as the case progressed to court, there was a sense of desperation in his eyes. We'll need a fortune to fight the charges, and all the while, Roger's own mother is more worried about her 70th birthday.

Ruth. She was a dreadful woman who spoke with her hands, rings clanking together like loose teeth. They were the first thing I noticed at our initial introduction all those years ago; a ruby, an emerald and a sapphire monstrosity that constantly clinked together. She quickly made it known she was keeper of the family fortune. Lately, she laughed away her oldest son's current predicament with a toss of her bleached blonde head.

Lifting the curtain, I looked across the yard at the solemn stone spire that was Thorpe Island Lighthouse. It stood sentinel-like, impossibly white against the grey blue sky. Gulls wheeled around the glass at its top, buffeted by the breeze. The idea of escaping to the one narrow sandy beach and drinking the weekend away was tempting but seemed less likely as the wind picked up. In the distance, I heard the waves crashing against the western cliff face.

I poured myself another shot.

Roger was suddenly next to me. "I'm going out for a walk," he said.

It was a statement not an invitation. I slid my hand around my frosted glass. "Sure."

And so he left. I was worried, obviously, as he hadn't completed unpacking our bag, which for a perfectionist like Roger is very unusual. For a few minutes, I rustled through the clothing, finding it hard to believe I had agreed to this whole charade of happy family.

It was four years ago that Ruth first commented on my drinking. Oh so nicely, of course, but then she never knew her darling son had taken a lover after my miscarriage.

Roger's silly mistake was long over now, but the repercussions remain. I guess I have taken a lover as well, his name is Johnnie Walker. We had a pattern the three of us; me, Johnnie and Roger. It was comfortable in its own way, but Ruth insisted on meddling.

I considered unpacking the rest of the bag but the veranda beckoned me, a rickety chair just asking to be sat in.

I decided to take the opportunity to relax for a moment and went outside. In an instant, I was aware of Ruth's figure towering in the distance, standing on the lighthouse lookout, her ridiculous fake platinum hair buffeted in the island air. She was staring into the distance at first; probably lost in memories of childhood stories she constantly regaled us about. She really could ruin any situation.

I sat heavily into the chair and couldn't help but look up at her. This weekend was going to be a long one. The next minute, the plump body of my mother-in-law plummeted briefly through the air before landing with a sickening thump on the sand.

It surprised me so much I almost spilled my drink.

STATEMENT OF FRAN CRISP

The last time I saw my mother-in-law before we boarded the boat to Thorpe Island was about a week ago. Ruth was dropped from the bowling team again and couldn't wait to share her woes with me. She told me all about Rene Graham calling her a cheat and complained about Dorry Peters who wouldn't let her correct the bias of her bowl in some competition. Blah, blah, blah.

Julie says I humour Ruth too much and that's why I get all the sob stories. Julie says she learnt long ago that once she brought out her bottle of scotch, Ruth would head to the door as though the very presence of alcohol might affect her some way.

But, being a listener has its advantages. That's how I learned more about Ruth's visit to the solicitor, ensuring her money went straight to Roger and Pete. Fine by me, I've never had any need for material things anyway. Pete and I first met at a psychic convention. He attended as a way to annoy his mother who had always been a smothering influence, despite the fact he was in his mid-twenties at that stage.

Pete's family has never been easy. Roger is a bore, Julie's a drunk, but they all pale in significance to Ruth. She thought my psychic ability was ridiculous and that's fine, not everyone has a gift or chooses to believe those who do.

Pete has his mother's looks. Natural dark hair (though his hasn't been transformed by a packet of dye) and probing blue eyes (though his don't look for chances to criticise). He works in finance, a dreadfully respectable job for the person I met all those years ago.

Anyway, last week when she called by, Ruth was eager to share more childhood memories with me. But, with a full weekend at Thorpe Island coming up, I didn't feel my usual need to indulge my mother-in-law. I thought I knew the one sure way to get rid of her.

"Ruth, can I read your tarot cards?" I asked.

To my surprise she agreed. Either she was humouring me for the sake of her son or the dumping from the bowling club had affected her more than I thought. I made a mental note to share this with Julie on the phone later — as long as I called her before 6:00 p.m. After that she was with Johnnie.

Ruth's ring encrusted fingers cut the deck of cards, and I lay three out in front of her.

"You know I don't believe in this stuff, Fran," she said unnecessarily.

"I know, but thank you for letting me practice."

What a soft touch. I could hear Pete's voice already. *No wonder she drops in all the time.* And only this morning Julie and I had been discussing Ruth's annoying insistence that we provide a grandchild for her.

This veiled threat of lawyers and money was probably some kind of emotional blackmail. But children have never been my bag, and as for Roger and Julie, I find it hard to believe someone as uptight as Roger could even have sex.

In view of this, I was surprised when I turned Ruth's first card over.

"Six of Cups, this card symbolises children."

Ruth smiled smugly. "Could be a sign for you Fran?"

Refraining myself from comment, I turned the next card over on the wooden table.

"Four of Swords — revenge," I announced.

"A sign for those old cows at the bowling club I'd say," Ruth huffed.

The third card showed its face beneath my hand.

"A lighthouse," Ruth exclaimed. "Well, that is prophetic, what with us heading to Thorpe Island."

No point in explaining the pictures symbolised something far deeper than the colourful images. I must admit though, I was relieved that the cards did their trick and Ruth got up to leave.

It wasn't till I unpacked my bag in the Thorpe Island hut that I recalled how unsettled Ruth had been as she walked out our kitchen door.

I should have realised earlier. In hindsight, I should have understood the strange feeling that came upon me as we lugged our cases along the sandy track. Instead, I put it down to queasiness from the boat ride.

Impulsively, I grabbed my tarot cards, the first thing I unpacked and set on the bedside table. Rifling through them, I picked out the three cards Ruth had chosen last week and threw them on the bed; Six of Cups, Tower Card, Four of Swords.

How stupid had I been to not interpret them as a group! At the time, I was in too much of a hurry to get Ruth out of our house.

I tossed the pack on the table and urgently flung open the door, its handle hitting the wooden wall with a dull thud. Julie was on the veranda of the next-door cabin, mouth open and glass in hand. I followed her gaze in time to see our mother-in-law plummeting to earth — her life had been extinguished merely 20 metres away.

STATEMENT OF DR ROGER CRISP

I was walking around the Island when Mum fell from the lighthouse. I've had a lot of things on my mind lately and Mum always said the sea air is good for clearing your soul.

You try coping with an alcoholic wife and a malpractice suit. Those two things must top the stress scale — up there with divorce and death I'd say. I've got death ticked off now and maybe divorce isn't far behind.

I'm used to plenty of death in my job of course. You become numb to it, and it's often the best thing for the patient, to be honest. But you're never used to the emotion of the ones left behind, especially when there's a baby involved.

You've probably heard about the malpractice suit? A young mother haemorrhaged during an emergency caesarean. I tidied that up well enough, delivered the little boy and stitched the mother back together. I got plenty of slaps on the back for that one.

Didn't realise the instrument that released her baby from its warm enclosure had accidentally nicked her bowel. While she learned to breastfeed her new child, an innocuous and tiny cut festered and poisoned her from the inside.

Malpractice suit; problem number one, and now this. The police say they aren't sure Mum wasn't pushed. Julie and Fran say they could see each other as her body plunged through the air and so they were counted out immediately. Pete says he was somewhere else on the island, but I didn't see him.

Once the police found out Mum planned to change her will they've been all over us. *Do we have money troubles?* As if they didn't know.

My mother was irritating and intrusive and I needed her money. But I didn't push her from that lighthouse.

In fact, I wish I had jumped myself.

STATEMENT OF PETER CRISP

My mother was always a selfish woman, but I did love her. It was Fran and I who indulged all those stories about her childhood. Just last week, Fran had to listen to the stories of Mum's holidays with Uncle Stan and Sophie, not to mention the dramas at the bowling club.

Not sure why we agreed to make the trip for the weekend, we're not what you would call a close family. Fran and Julie get on, but any conversation with Julie has to be made early in the day or, as she admits, it's more like talking to her scotch bottle.

As for my brother, we've never been close; he was the scholar, and I was the dreamer. I only stick to my finance job as a way to pay the bills. And, while on the subject of money, we don't need any, thanks very much. Mum could have left her money to an African rhinoceros' sanctuary for all I care.

I remember Uncle Stan. Though I was pretty young, we saw a lot of him when he left his post at Thorpe Island as the longest serving lighthouse keeper. I remember him as a tall man with piercing blue eyes, often around at our house for a home brew beer on a Sunday afternoon. He never talked about Thorpe Island though. Not surprising really as his only daughter died there.

When I told Fran that after Mum was over the other day, her face went taut and drained of colour.

"That's terrible," she said. "What happened?"

"She fell from the top of the light. She was still alive when she hit the ground, but apparently but not for long. It's hard to get medical help in such an isolated place, especially back then."

I shrugged but didn't mean to sound heartless. It's just that the story of Mum's cousin Sophie is one Roger and I have grown up with and heard repeatedly for years, followed by much anguished turning of the rings that decorated her fingers.

"Having children is just asking for heartache," Fran said sadly "That poor man, alone on an island with his dead child."

"Oh, he wasn't alone," I said. "Mum was there on holidays. I'm surprised she never mentioned that part of the drama to you."

I relayed the familiar story. "They were playing hide and seek, Mum was off hiding and Sophie must have leant over too far. Mum said she stayed hidden until she heard Uncle Stan wailing in grief."

Fran shuddered.

Freakish to think that history has now repeated itself.

The police say they suspect it may not have been an accident. I don't know about that, but I'll tell you one thing for sure.

I did not kill my mother.

Statement of Sophie Anderson (deceased)

I've been waiting for Ruthie to come back and visit.

I've been alone with the terns as they fly back each winter, drifting through the clumps of trees that group together in green secrecy in the middle of the island. It's been a long time. But I remember that day as though it was yesterday.

It was a beautiful sunny afternoon, a slight breeze threatening to blow up from the west. Dad spent the morning polishing the glass of the light while all around him the ocean tossed and waved its white caps at us.

"Sophie," he said to me after lunch, "Why don't you show Ruth the cave on Hopalong Beach."

150

I avoided his gaze at first, but Ruthie's insistence wore me down. She was my hero after all. She was almost two years older than me and lived on the mainland, that faraway place where the world didn't drift by without notice.

My hair was ruffled in the wind as we walked; our voices carried along the beach, scooting along the sand on the breeze.

My cousin always brought exciting stories from the mainland. She talked of friends at school and fancy clothes. There was usually nothing new from me, not a thing I could impress her with. But now there was something I needed to show her. Excitement bubbled through me.

It was ironic that Dad suggested we go into that cave as that was where I hid my most treasured possession.

Ruth's eyes opened wide when I showed her the sapphire ring. My ten-year-old heart swelled. I had impressed her at last.

"A sailor gave it to me," I said. "He more or less washed up on the beach last winter. He said he owed his life to us and Thorpe Island."

The deep blue trinket sparkled in spite of the dull light of the cave. Ruth looked impressed, then excited and then calculating, although I didn't recognise that expression back then.

"I think you should give it to me Sophie, I can show everyone back on the mainland. I'll say it's yours of course."

Our eyes met then. I clasped the ring in my hand and shook my head.

A smile set on Ruthie's face.

"Never mind," she said. "Hide and seek. Let's play that Soph."

And so, we returned to the lighthouse. I was grateful she had let me conceal the sapphire back into the rock crevice. Glad that she understood that I also deserved something special in life.

We climbed the lighthouse's 93 steps. Dad had finished

polishing and the glass of the light shone in the late morning sun.

On the top railing, the wind whipped our hair across our faces; the horizon seemed to stretch forever. "You go first," she said.

Suddenly, I knew what she planned to do — sneak back to the cave and steal my treasure! I had to buy time so I could move the sapphire ring.

"No, you go first," I insisted.

We argued, in a childish way, and I'll never truly know if Ruthie meant to push me over the edge or if it was an accident, but the last thing I heard was the clatter of her shoes as she rushed down the lighthouse steps and right past my crumpled body. I knew exactly where she was going.

The thing about a life in limbo is you have a long time to observe and think. I've seen the way she coddled her sons, children I would never have the opportunity to have.

I saw my dad, her Uncle Stan, wither away in the suburbs, while I remained drawn back to the island that had always been our home.

I witnessed Ruthie badger her daughters-in-law, and though they have faults of their own, they never measured up in selfishness to my cousin Ruth.

I willed her up those steps today, following behind her like a breath of wind; a force of nature that never dies. When we got to the top, my chance had finally come.

Ruthie's back was not the supple, lithe board that it had been in her youth. For a moment I was shocked at the contrast to my hand, still that of a child and frozen in time after all these years. How had she lived with herself? Carrying around that ring on her finger, truly believing nothing was ever her fault.

I'm not unfair, I sent a sign. Mind you, it was through tarot cards, and maybe deep inside I knew Ruthie would never heed their message. At that last minute, when I thrust my arm forward, Fran was looking at the Tower Card down on the ground below. I saw her face as she realised it depicted a person plummeting from a lighthouse.

I will never meet Ruthie's family in person, but I have now set them all free. It's not too late, and they will have her money. May their lives go in the directions they choose.

It's a restless spirit that finds no resolution. But now I am also free.

See the light, see the light ... I always pleaded with Ruth to do that. And maybe, as she plummeted into the ground of my island home, that's exactly what she finally did.

GIVING IT YOUR BEST SHOT

The fabric sign on the Welsh Arms Hotel was affixed to the ornate iron fence with coloured wire and gently swaying balloons, which bobbed around in the afternoon breeze. Tony could tell it had been put up with a flourish, each balloon at a different height. Exactly what one would expect from a group of artists. Curled lettering indicated its importance cheerfully to Tony, and he instantly knew he was in the right place.

Western Australian Photographer's Conference.

Inside the pub door, the atmosphere was buzzing. Several groups of men were leaning into each other in earnest conversation, hands moving in staccato fashion to prove their point. There were women too of course; the art of photography didn't discriminate by gender. Along the panelled wall were a series of large prints. Tony admired them briefly.

He had a quick mind and decided almost immediately which was his favourite photograph. It wasn't the panoramic landscapes that stretched with the dull brilliance of the Australian bush or the shadow play of evening in a pine forest, dramatic as they were. It was the image hanging second from the end that really caught his attention — a wild rabbit, frozen in a mid-air leap, the whites of its eyes angled back in terror to something just out of the frame. Yep, that's the one that appeals to my artistic sense, Tony thought with a small smile. He had seen it before of course.

Tony grabbed a quick beer — straight draught, no craft beer, thanks very much. Turning from the barman's suggestion of Wild Elk or Top Notch Ale, he literally ran into photographer, Curtis Potter, the very person he hoped to come across.

Potter was a big man, with shoulders more suggestive of a football player than a photographer. The giveaway was the intentness of his facial expression, as though his eyes were trained to scrutinise every detail of any object that came into his visual field. In this case, it was Tony.

"Curtis Potter," Tony extended his hand. "It's such a pleasure to meet you. My name is Tony Janson."

Accustomed to being recognised, Curtis shook Tony's hand briskly. From what Tony had learned, Curtis was the reason this annual get together was so well attended. A local hero whose skilful photography had given him a worldwide reputation that others could only dream of. Tony liked to consider himself a professional as well and refused to be daunted by this artist's obvious self-confidence.

"I love your rabbit photo," Tony said. It was true, he did. "It captures great expression in an animal subject," he continued, hoping to sound passably knowledgeable.

Curtis looked over at the wall, again with that stare of intense examination as though he was viewing it for the first time. "Wild Flight? Thank you. I won a trophy from National Geographic for that one a few years ago."

"I have a few trophies at home too," Tony said, quickly annoyed he felt the need to compete.

Curtis raised an eyebrow. "Tell me, what would you have shot that with? What lens is the most useful in your repertoire?"

Tony was an astute judge of the nuances of emotion, something that always came in handy. He felt anger swell in his chest at what he interpreted as condescension. In spite of what he'd been told, he hadn't expected to dislike Curtis so quickly. With a practiced smile, the feeling was quickly quelled, never transferring to a single muscle in his face.

Tony considered the question for a moment. He looked at the photo of the leaping rabbit, observing the naked fear in its eyes. The animal was unaware there was no threat of actual harm. But for the unsuspecting creature, how often was that not the case?

"Adaptive zoom maybe? Yep, I think that would give the best shot. You can get up close, wouldn't miss anything."

Curtis gave a distracted nod, his attention already elsewhere. "Well, good luck with your work in the future."

Tony nodded as Curtis moved on. He remained in the bar for a moment longer, thoughtfully downing the last froth of his beer, watching as Curtis handed a drink to the redhead in the corner, his hand brushing her right breast ever so briefly as he passed the glass of wine to her.

Teresa had been right. What an arsehole.

Outside the Welsh Arms, Tony grabbed his equipment from the car he had stolen earlier. The brown bag was heavy and cumbersome. He was getting too old for this shit.

Nestling himself behind a leafy bush across the road from the pub, careful not to be seen, Tony set up his tripod, ready to shoot his latest subject. Over his life, he had learned he was capable of a lot of things, but one thing he prided himself on was his honesty. To a certain extent anyway.

For example, the adaptive zoom was certainly the most

useful lens he had, and when Curtis walked jauntily out the front door of the Welsh Arms about twenty minutes later, Tony would also prove that it really did ensure you didn't miss anything.

Tony was a shooter alright, just not the sort that Curtis assumed.

The loud bang was something he had never gotten used to, he admitted to Curtis' wife later. They were gulping on beers beneath Tony's trophies in the lounge room: the stuffed heads of a stag from Canada and a zebra from a trip to Africa the previous summer. The television blared in front of them, the national news leading with the story of the unknown sniper shot that killed a famous international photographer on the streets of Perth.

"But anyway Teresa, let me tell you a joke," Tony insisted, the day's work already in the past.

She rolled her eyes.

"No, no, love, it's hilarious, just wait."

"Two shooters walk into a bar ... "

CHINESE WHISPERS

It was lunchtime on Tuesday and along the mauve carpeted corridor of Santana Court Nursing Home, which stretched to the western end of town, the residents moved at varying paces towards the dining room.

The neatly-spaced paintings they shuffled past were all dedicated to dear departed residents. Each meticulously cleaned and disinfected picture hung mutely on the hallway wall and supposedly related the character of the deceased. Hence, in the tiny farming community of Golden Hills, there was a predominance of country landscapes for the men, while framed pastel flowers were the flavour for the ladies.

In the communal dining room, which opened at the end of the corridor, a scattering of pink Laminex tables, each neatly arranged with four grey chairs and a vase of silk flowers, silently oversaw the daily comings and goings of the 34 residents.

Nance Wilson sat alone at one of these tables. She had on beige pants and a floral shirt bought by her daughter-in-law. Her hair was piled up high on her head in a messy grey haystack. It had been fastened with far too many bobby pins than she thought necessary by the early shift girls, and it was giving her a slight headache. They were lazy girls, generally rushing through their jobs and chatting over head as though she didn't exist.

Nance kept her thoughts to herself these days, preferring not to communicate with the dithering fools of the Nursing Home — and that was only the staff!

Her watery blue eyes rested with some satisfaction on the hydrangea outside the window. Although the tinted glass dulled the colour and the pink bloom nodded silently in the breeze, courtesy of the soundproofing, Nance obtained a pleasure from it that was lost in the apricot silk atrocity in the vase in front of her.

"Now Nance, dear, it's time for your lunch."

Helen Lennox slid a bowl in front of Nance with the premise of delivering some fantastic delicacy. Helen was a dried-up little woman, youngish, Nance supposed, but then anyone under 75 was young to Nance these days. She bustled around the Home with far more importance than necessary for the kitchen help. Nance's lips pursed slightly. At least in her day, everyone knew their place in the world. When she had worked behind the shop counter as a young woman, she would never have dared to overstep her mark.

Her eyes remained determinedly on the garden outside. It was Tuesday after all, and that could only mean ...

"Bean casserole," Helen said brightly, slipping a spoon into the papery skin of Nance's fingers, "Plenty of iron to keep you going through bingo tomorrow!"

Steak also has plenty of iron, Nance retorted in her head, but the thoughts rarely transformed into words anymore, well, not in the way she wanted, and so she sat silently, a gentle smile on her lips.

"Patricia not in for a visit today?" Helen asked, nudging Nance's chair slightly closer to the table.

Nance chose not to think of her daughter-in-law. Instead, her attention was drawn to a noise from the kitchen area, a persistent banging, followed by the appearance of a sack truck that had certainly seen better days. The way the man clattered and banged through the door it was little wonder there was barely a scratch of red paint left on it. Once he'd righted his truck and adjusted the pants that hung down far lower than was decent, he turned toward the dining area, a too easy grin appearing on his face. Nance felt Helen stiffen by her side and her attention heightened at this unusual intrusion into the daily routine of Santana.

"Afternoon, Helen," the man said, "just delivering the groceries."

Nance was used to being ignored and took the opportunity to study the intruder. The man had a dumpiness about him that overtook his height. With his black hair and large nose, he reminded Nance somewhat of penguin, and a clumsy one at that. When he spoke, there was a sharpness to the curve of his mouth that prickled at Nance's memory.

"Can't get out the back exit," the man explained. "The doors had it. There's tradesmen fixing the tradesman's exit."

He laughed at his own humour and Helen responded with a tight-lipped smile. The man bundled his sack truck outside the side door to the garden, bumping into a dining chair on the way.

"Need a license for this I reckon," he said brightly.

Nance saw the coldness of Helen's gaze as the man shut the door.

The sedate atmosphere of the dining room seemed to recover itself as he left. Helen was prompted back into action and moved Nance's bowl closer to her as though that could make the bean casserole more appetising.

"Heath Whittle has a lot to answer for," Helen hissed at Nance. "He should learn to live up to his promises."

As if on cue, a delivery truck revved its engine and then appeared at the end of the driveway; a modern, fancy vehicle, chugging impatiently as it waited to turn onto the road.

"Suppose I should be impressed with the new truck, not to mention his new car. Not likely Nance."

Nance knew Helen didn't expect a reply but her mind buzzed with a million questions over this unexpected development. *Heath Whittle.* No wonder that beak-like nose had seemed familiar. She'd known his grandfather Sam, and that man, too, was a snake.

Helen, however, had other animals in mind.

"Take my word for it, Mrs Wilson, that man is a rat."

Remembering her dealings with Sam Whittle, Nance didn't doubt it for a second and as Helen moved through the door to rustle the other residents along the hallway, Nance looked down drearily at her bean casserole.

In her heyday, Pat Stead was chairperson of the Golden Hills Council. That was before the council amalgamated with three other nearby towns and lost all its local importance. Still, 11 years at the top of the small pond left Pat with an air of superiority that never quite left her gingery head. She paraded around Santana like the belle of the ball, humouring a host of less luminary associates.

It was true, Pat probably was the most competent resident of them all but then her influence over Ivan Pfeiffer, former councillor with whom she'd carried on many late meetings, helped her secure a place in Santana, way before it was really necessary. Of course, it wasn't as though her son, Rod, really wanted her to vacate the family home for him and Rosanna, his new bride. As she told anyone who would listen, the decision to move to Santana and be of assistance to residents and staff alike at Santana had been entirely hers.

Pat quelled her annoyance by patting her styled coiffure on entering the dining room. The regular hairdresser, Madeline, had been off sick, and the other girl, rarely did her hair as well; the air-conditioning was harsh enough on her hair as it was.

To make matters worse, that old dear, Nance Wilson, was sitting in the only seat away from the blast of the ducted air. Her daughter Rose was due for a visit after lunch, and her hair was almost at the point of collapse already! Pat stroked it gently. Well, it wasn't as if Nance would interrupt her lunch for a chat, poor dear, and with a deep breath of martyrdom, Pat headed for that exact table where Nance sat, bean casserole untouched.

"Bean casserole again," she harrumphed, "it must be Tuesday."

Nance shifted her eyes slightly to take in the pompous figure of Pat Whittle. More iron in steak, she thought, but even had she been able to form the words, there was little chance Pat would listen. She was already off like a two-bob watch.

"I don't know why they think we're satisfied with that," Pat ranted, taking a seat opposite to Nance and again surveying her plate with disdain. "The kitchen budget needs a complete over-haul with some inside advice as to what we would like. Don't you think Nance?"

Nance knew her opinion wasn't really being sought and kept quiet.

"Beef stew," Pat went on with relish. "That's what I used to like on the farm. The whole family loved beef stew on Fridays."

Pat's bean casserole arrived and was placed in front of her.

Nance smiled inwardly at the fact that Helen rushed off quickly before Pat could draw breath. It made Nance think of the earlier departure of Heath Whittle.

Pat looked at Nance suddenly, sensing an unusual sharpness in her eyes, and to Pat's utter surprise, Nance's dry lips parted and she began to speak. At first it was an undiscernible mumble.

"What was that dear?" Pat asked indulgently, hiding her surprise at Nance's attempt to communicate.

"There's been a rat in the kitchen."

The fork that had been clenched in Pat's leathery hand dropped in a horrified clatter on the grey Laminex.

"A rat! Did you see it?" Pat asked breathlessly.

Nance thought of the pointed nose and slippery manner of Heath Whittle. She summoned her strength. "Absolutely."

Pat's eyes grew wide with alarm and she pushed her plate away with an air of disgust. She stirred with the resolve that kept her at the head of the council table for so many years.

"That's inappropriate," Pat said with well-practised tact. "Something needs to be done about this."

But, exhausted from her efforts, Nance appeared to have nodded off, her head gently bobbing as she breathed in the aroma of bean casserole and dreamt about a dinner of steak.

Rose Patterson drove her red sedan neatly into the parking space outside Santana Court and looked at the figures arranged like statues behind the tinted glass and supressed a shiver.

"Don't you ever shove me into one of those places," she said regularly to her husband James after her weekly visit to her mother. "I'd rather go straight to the cemetery." Rose stretched her long legs out onto the asphalt and stood up, grasping the bag of liquorice allsorts her mother always requested 'to get her by'.

This week, she'd grabbed two bags, mainly out of guilt for missing yesterday's visit. James was hosting a barbecue for some work associates tonight at their house. Rose had found herself up to her neck in cheesecake and marinade all day yesterday before she realised the time.

And now, by the look of the line-up of chairs, Rose was about to interrupt the weekly bingo game. She gritted her teeth as she pushed her way through the heavy front door; she was a fully grown woman and wife of the grain silo manager but her larger-than-life mother still reduced her to a five-year-old.

Rose found Pat in her regular position for bingo. Near the front, but a little to the left, right where she could be the most help, she confided to Rose. Naturally, her hearing was much better than many of the other old dears, and she liked to be able to yell out the number for those at the back, although most of them, like Nance, used the back row as the chance for a small nap. After all, they had no choice whether to be in there or not, having been brought in seated in wheelchairs.

Today she looked distracted, Rose thought, surveying the gingery head of her mother, although she brightened on catching sight of Rose and the liquorice allsorts.

"You'll have to do without me today love," Pat said. "My daughter's here."

Rose smiled at Kathy, the nurse currently employed in rolling bingo numbers in a wire ball.

"That's fine Pat. You have a nice visit."

Rose was surprised to find her mother gleaming like an excited school girl once they got to her room, with not even a mention of Rose's absence the day before. Pat lowered herself into a chair, taking the lolly packets as she did so and tossing then onto the bed. Rose stared at them in surprise.

"Mum, are you feeling okay?"

Pat held up one hand airily. "Fine, dear. I just have a bit of news to share." She leaned over conspiratorially, rolling the words in her mouth like a boiled lolly. "Actually, it's some gossip."

Rose smiled. "Don't tell me Mr Potter has run off with Doris Gardener?" On every visit, Rose imagined a Potter and Gardener would be a good mix, but the joke was lost on her mother.

"It was Nance Wilson who told me. You know old Nance, never says a word, poor pet." Pat paused and took her daughter's silence as not understanding.

"You remember Nance, Rose? She used to work down the street when you were a girl. You were terrified of her most of the time. Not a bad old stick though, really, and a real pillar of the community in her time."

A smile rested on Rose's lips as she listened to her mother, but her mind was running through the array of salads she'd prepared for the evening and whether there would be enough. Luckily, women can multitask, she thought, reaching over to wipe dust from the top of the frame that held a photo of James, Rose and their two children.

Pat had paused from her biography of Nance Wilson and opened a pack of liquorice, offering one to her daughter.

Rose popped one in her mouth. "So, what did Mrs Wilson tell you?"

"She said ... " Pat trailed off, the excitement of keeping the titbit of news in her mind for a day had momentarily taken over what the news actually was. "Oh bother, what was it?"

Rose waited patiently. The forgetfulness of her mother was becoming a more and more frequent part of their visits.

"What?" she prompted gently.

"A rat," Pat said at last, lifting her chin triumphantly.

"There was a rat in the kitchen. It was in the beans. Nance saw the thing herself."

Rose stopped mid chew. "A rat? That's disgusting. Is she sure?"

Pat was wound up now, boosted by the fact that her memory hadn't totally deserted her. "Absolutely, she said. I remember every word. A rat in the kitchen in the beans."

"But don't you have bean casserole ... "

"Every Tuesday," Pat finished. She puffed up like a rooster, harking back to her days as Golden Hills council chairperson. "Now, Rose, what are we going to do about it?"

"I'll speak to James, Mum. Don't worry, we'll sort something out."

On Manion Street, Golden Hills, the fairy lights twinkled, the barbecue sizzled and the array of salads bought gasps of admiration from the guests.

Rose, on her third glass of wine, stood in the corner of her garden, under the bottlebrush, and scanned her guests: the twelve employees of the Golden Hills Silos and their partners. After his recent promotion to manager of the facility, James had been determined to hold a barbie to show his mates he was still the same old bloke. By the way the beers were disappearing from the esky and the typical male circle that held sway at barbecues broke into hearty laughter every few minutes, Rose figured he was fairly safe.

Rose had known everyone assembled in her garden for several years, although none of them were close friends, so as moral support she had invited her good friend, Belinda. When Belinda had arrived earlier in the evening, Rose had detected the red eyes and worn expression that could only mean she had endured another fight with her husband, Mike. Their stoushes were legendary among their friends, caused in no small part by Belinda's flirtatiousness. Belinda had tearfully confided to Rose that Mike accused her of going out too much when he attended a conference out of town, mandatory for his position on the local council.

"I didn't want to eat home alone," she told Rose over a strong cup of coffee. "What's wrong with a meal at the pub?"

"Nothing," Rose had replied. "If you'd eaten alone."

"Tom was by himself too. He was in the bar, it made sense for us to eat together."

"Maybe to you Belinda, but not to Mike."

As penance, Rose noticed Belinda had spent most of the night talking to her daughter in the sandpit. Mike was entrenched in the men's circle, which was only broken by the occasional trip to the esky.

Rose sipped on her wine and caught the eye of James as he rolled the sausages with practiced ease on the hotplate. She loved her husband dearly, and the three glasses of wine made him seem even more attractive.

Meat sizzled on the barbecue. Rose walked over to it, leaning in to inhale the fumes while placing a hand on her husband's shoulder.

"Smells good."

James smiled, "Everything seems to be okay," he commented, "and Belinda is on her best behaviour. What's the story there?"

Rose gave her husband a quick version of the afternoon's teary conversation. James nodded and began to pile meat on the serving tray.

"Mike's under a bit of stress at work as well," he said. "The powers that be don't seem to think he's pulling his weight."

Rose was dying to know more, but at that moment, one of

the other men arrived to ferry one of the meat trays to the outdoor table.

"Looks good James," someone commented.

"Don't you love the way they stand around, then take all the credit for the cooking." It was Belinda's voice, aided by several glasses of wine.

"Not at all," James said jovially. "Rose deserves all the credit."

He dug into one of the glass bowls on the table. "And this salad is always my favourite."

Rose almost laughed. "Bean salad. You better not let Mum hear you say that."

"Hasn't she forgiven you visiting a day late?"

"It's not that. She said Nance Wilson saw a rat in the beans in the kitchen."

Belinda interrupted, glass almost at her lips. "At Santana? That's terrible."

James looked sceptical. "Is she sure? Nance isn't exactly the full quid these days, and actually, neither is your mother."

Rose swatted him good naturedly. "She's positive, and as Mum said, 'Nance was a pillar of the community once.'"

"No wonder Heath is driving around in a new car and putting on an extension to his house," Belinda put in. "He's selling contaminated beans to the nursing home and no doubt charging them a fortune!"

"Well, there's not much opposition is there? I mean, the butcher shop is the only other place in town that sells any type of food," James commented.

"True, but Noel has fruit and veg and other stuff in his butcher shop as well these days." Rose said. "Only yesterday when I bought the barbie meat, I got my salad gear and dips in there as well."

James grabbed his beer with his spare hand. "Well,

someone should check it out," he said, ready to return to his workmates. "There doesn't need to be false rumours bouncing around the town."

At 2:00 am, Belinda Newton woke up with a thumping headache. In the modern brick home at the end of Frome Street, she threw back the quilt, padded down the hallway and searched the kitchen cupboard for painkillers. She'd spent almost the entire party chatting to a four-year-old and still managed to get a hangover.

The search was fruitless and she settled for a glass of water, which she drank slowly, staring out the window to the moonless night.

"You shouldn't drink so much wine."

Mike's voice came from the doorway. He stood with one arm stretched up the doorframe and was silhouetted by the light that came down the hallway from their bedroom.

Belinda grimaced and put down her glass. "No, I shouldn't drink so much cheap wine. Rose did warn me."

Something tweaked at the edge of Belinda's brain. It was the foggy memory of their earlier argument and the way she had decided to make amends.

"I heard something tonight that you might find handy to know at work."

Mike tilted his head sceptically.

"Oh yeah? What?"

"You might want to haul your health inspection team over Whittle's store. Apparently, the food's contaminated and making everyone ill at the nursing home."

Mike's eyebrows lifted as he absorbed the information.

Belinda searched her brain, sure there was another snippet in there.

"And he's had cheques bouncing too. All around town, James said."

"Well, the way Heath has been spending money lately I'm not surprised. Do you know he's sponsoring the footy team to the tune of a thousand bucks?"

Belinda whistled in the dark kitchen and said in a low voice, "Do you know how good springing him would look for you?"

Mike pictured his boss's face when he uncovered such a small-town scandal. The trouble was, as a council health inspector, everything had to be done by the book, which meant forms, arranged interviews and inspections. Plenty of time for Heath to clean up the shop. Mike needed the kudos, but he had to be sure.

"Thanks, hon," Mike said, kissing his wife on the top of her head. "I'll check it out."

Late Friday evening when most of Golden Hills attended the local basketball games or held up the front bar of the pub, Mike Newton took his dog for a walk. Harry, the retriever, looked doubtful at first, the clink of his leash had been an unfamiliar sound for some months.

As the residents of Santana Nursing Home were settled into their beds for the night, Mike went out into the cool night air, ridiculously grateful for the lack of moonlight. He saun-tered along the footpath, letting Harry sniff at every post along the way, occasionally waving to a car while keeping his eye on Whittle's Store at the end of the street. It was dark so he couldn't recognise the driver of any vehicle, but a wave hello was just the way a small town worked.

It had been another slow day at work. Mike had decided they lived in the cleanest and healthiest place on earth, with little to do but the regular mundane chores. Which was why, with a clandestine pang of excitement, Mike approached Heath Whittle's store, his heart beating wildly.

Still on the opposite side of the road, Mike stood in front of Noel's butchers and feigned interest in the display. To the right of the door was a plaque indicating the building had housed the first shop in the district. Mike read with feigned interest about the self-taught butcher whose wife stood at the counter for more years than most could remember. The back of the brightly lit shop showed a display of fresh vegetable and jars of continental goods, but Mike's attention was on the huge cuts of meat displayed in the refrigerated counter.

"Now that's what I call real food, Harry."

Harry wagged his tail, basking in the sudden onset of attention, but his master was now staring across the street. Whittle's Store was also illuminated, aisles of packets and tins secure under the fluorescent light. Heath's van was not in the driveway.

As casually as he could, Mike crossed the deserted street. He felt his pocket, his hand resting on the shape of the torch and felt like he was part of some surreal movie. The streets and roads were deserted. He had about half an hour before the exodus from the local basketball stadium would see an increase in traffic. Mike strolled up the empty driveway, thankful the hum of the external refrigerator motors covered the crunch of his steps.

The backyard, such as it was, was overgrown with weeds at the edges of a cursorily mown patch of green. Plastic milk crates and pieces of snail-eaten rubbish littered the small yard. Heath's new found wealth apparently didn't extend into landscaping. The windows were high and rectangular and appeared to be covered in cardboard from the inside, though an eerie glow of the security lights came through one corner.

Mike retrieved a crate from the clutches of the growing grass and placed it on level ground. He put his phone in to photo mode — he intended to have proof of any health issues before arranging an inspection. He had been caught before by the council's protocol of arranging an inspection time. As if Heath would bring out the rats for the council's visit! Mike grimaced, no wonder his job was so difficult.

Harry sniffed around the yard with great interest as Mike balanced on the crate and peered into the small patch of light, camera at the ready. What he saw took his breath away.

"Heath, you rotter," Mike whispered to himself, aiming the lens through the tiny opening and clicking away. Still balancing on the crate, Mike shook his head as he reviewed the incriminating photographs. Retrieving Harry's lead, he leant down to rub the dog's head.

"Come on Harry, walk's over; I know someone who'll be very interested in these photos."

Mike retraced the path to his house. The occasional car passed by now and then, and he lifted one arm in greeting, the other had the leash looped around his wrist and his hand tightly around the camera in his pocket. Once at the corner, Mike got out his mobile phone and made a call.

The whole of Golden Hills was roused by a police siren early on Saturday morning. From the nursing home, Nance and Pat lifted their heads from breakfast. Though the soundproof glass kept out the noise, the flashing lights quickly caught their interest.

"What's that about then, Nance?" Pat asked rhetorically, as for the second time in less than a week, they again shared a table.

Nance couldn't imagine, and said so, though her mumbled

words were lost in Pat's habit of holding a conversation with herself.

"A bit of excitement for Golden Hills, eh?" she told her poached eggs.

"What the hell is that noise?" Rose said, neither lifting her head from her pillow nor opening her eyes.

The siren quietened as it took the turn into Main Street. James, his legs still aching from umpiring basketball the night before, barely moved beneath the quilt. "Guess we'll find out later," Rose said, rolling over away from the clock which silently flicked over to 8:03 am.

Harry the dog, wagging his tail with excitement over his second walk in less than 24 hours looked at steaks in Noel's butcher shop window with uncontrolled enthusiasm. On the other end of the lead, Mike feigned surprise as a nearing police car pulled over at the general store. Senior Constable Edwards gave a barely discernible nod to Mike as he got out the car, strode to the still locked doors of the shop and rapped sharply on the glass.

Heath Whittle appeared with a jovial grin and worked at the locks, flinging the door wide.

"In a rush for the paper this morning, Jack?" Mike heard him say.

Mike didn't hear what Jack Edwards said next but the look on Heath's face spoke volumes.

It was Tuesday at the Golden Hills Nursing Home. The regular hairdresser had been and gone. Pat was expecting a visit from Rose after lunch. Nance sat at the table with the horrid silk flowers, a small smile resting on her lips.

At precisely 12 noon, Helen Lennox bustled out from the kitchen, balancing four plates on her chunky arms. She had seemed much brighter these last few days, Nance had noticed, and now as she placed the white plates onto the table, she was positively beaming.

"What, no bean casserole?" Pat said in surprise, looking at the small cut of meat in front of her as though it might disappear.

Nance lifted her head from where it rested almost on one shoulder, her milky eyes glistening with interest as she viewed her meal, her tastebuds stirring for the first time in years.

"You wouldn't believe it ladies, Whittle's Store has been closed down. All our supplies now come from Noel's — it's amazing what he stocks in that small store."

Pat, former councillor, needed to know details.

"What on earth happened?"

Helen leaned close, eager to share the story.

"Drugs! Can you believe it? Heath was growing a drug crop in the back room of the shop! The police received a tip-off, photos and all. Apparently, Mike Norton, he's the council health inspector you know, has been suspicious that something's been going on in there for quite a while. Goodness knows why."

"You know how things get around in a small town," Pat intoned.

"He's been in here as well, checked out the kitchen for some reason. He gave the place a clean bill of health, naturally."

Nance listened as they prattled on. Heath's new car and splashing the money around, suddenly all made sense it seemed. But Nance had heard enough, her mind wandered to other times, wafting along on the scent of the steak.

"Well Nance, what do you think?" Pat said once Helen had gone. "Nothing exciting ever happens here like that!"

But she wasn't listening. Nance Wilson, former proprietor of Golden Hills Meats and pillar of the community, was savouring the tiny cubes of steak.

Plenty of iron in steak; she had told her customers that for years, all the time staring across the road at the cheaply run business that belonged to Sam Whittle, a slimy rat of a man.

Now, why had she been thinking of him lately?

Dear reader,

We hope you enjoyed reading *She is Vengeance*. Please take a moment to leave a review, even if it's a short one. Your opinion is important to us.

Discover more books by Kristin Murdock at https://www.nextchapter.pub/authors/kristin-murdock

Want to know when one of our books is free or discounted? Join the newsletter at http://eepurl.com/bqqB3H

Best regards,

Kristin Murdock and the Next Chapter Team

She Is Vengeance
ISBN: 978-4-86750-791-9

Published by
Next Chapter
1-60-20 Minami-Otsuka
170-0005 Toshima-Ku, Tokyo
+818035793528

10th June 2021

.